ALSO BY MAGNUS MILLS

The Restraint of Beasts

ALL QUIET ON THE ORIENT EXPRESS

—— A NOVEL ——

MAGNUS MILLS

SCRIBNER PAPERBACK FICTION
PUBLISHED BY SIMON & SCHUSTER
NEW YORK LONDON TORONTO SYDNEY SINGAPORE

SCRIBNER PAPERBACK FICTION
Simon & Schuster, Inc.
Rockefeller Center
1230 Avenue of the Americas
New York, NY 10020

This book is a work of fiction. Names, characters, places, and incidents
either are products of the author's imagination or are used fictitiously.
Any resemblance to actual events or locales or persons, living or dead,
is entirely coincidental.

Copyright © 1999 by Magnus Mills

All rights reserved, including the right of reproduction in whole
or in part in any form.

First Scribner Paperback Fiction edition 2000
Originally published by Arcade Publishing, Inc., New York.
SCRIBNER PAPERBACK FICTION and design are trademarks
of Macmillan Library Reference USA, Inc., used under license
by Simon & Schuster, the publisher of this work.

Manufactured in the United States of America

1   3   5   7   9   10   8   6   4   2

Library of Congress Cataloging-in-Publication Data
Mills, Magnus.
All quiet on the Orient Express : a novel / Magnus Mills.
—1st Scribner pbk. fiction ed.
p.   cm.
1. Camp sites, facilities, etc.—Fiction. I. Title.
PR6063.I37784 A79 2000
823'.914—dc21   00-036521

ISBN 0-684-87168-8 (Pbk)

TO MY LOVING MOTHER

ALL QUIET ON
THE ORIENT EXPRESS

1

'I thought I'd better catch you before you go,' he said. 'Expect you'll be leaving today, will you?'

'Hadn't planned to,' I replied.

'A lot of people choose to leave on Monday mornings.'

'Well, I thought I'd give it another week, actually. The weather seems quite nice.'

'So you're staying on then?'

'If that's alright with you.'

'Of course it is,' he said. 'You're welcome to stay as long as you like.'

I'd been wondering when he would come to collect the rent. Several times in the past few days he'd gone round calling on everyone else, but for some reason he kept leaving me out. Now, on the sixth morning, he had finally made his approach. I emerged from my tent, barefoot, and the conversation continued.

'Nice place you've got here.'

'Yes,' he said. 'We like it very much. Of course, I've been here all my life, so I don't know any different.'

'Suppose not.'

'But everyone who comes here says they like it.'

'I'm not surprised.'

He opened the palm of his hand and for the first time I noticed he was holding a wooden tent peg.

'This yours?' he asked.

'No,' I said. 'Mine are all metal ones.'

'Do you want it? You can have it as a spare if you like.'

'Is it nobody else's?'

'There's no one else left,' he said. 'They've all gone.'

I glanced around the field. 'Oh yes, you're right. Shame really.'

'One speck of rain and they all flee. Then the sun comes back and they miss it.'

'That's always the way, isn't it?'

'Almost always. Do you want this then?'

'OK,' I said, taking the peg. 'Thanks.'

'Would you like to pay some rent?'

'Oh yes. How much do I owe you?'

He adopted a businesslike smile. 'It's a pound a night.'

'That's six pounds so far then.'

'If you've been here six nights, yes.'

'Right.' I took a five-pound note from my back pocket and handed it over, and then began fishing for some coins.

'That's quite expensive really, isn't it?' he remarked. 'Just for you, your tent and your motorbike.'

'Seems alright to me,' I replied.

'I ought to be giving you a bit of discount if you're staying another week.'

'A pound a night's fine,' I said, giving him the balance.

'Alright then,' he said. 'That's grand.'

Now that the transaction was over I expected him to make his excuses and move on, but after he'd taken the money he replanted his feet and looked up at the sky.

'On holiday, are you?' he asked.

'Not really,' I said. 'Well, sort of.'

He smiled again. 'Which?'

'Well, I'm between things at the present. I've been working all summer to save some money so I can go East during the winter.'

'You mean the east coast?'

'Oh, no,' I said. 'Sorry. Abroad East. You know, Turkey, Persia, and then overland to India.'

'I see,' he said, nodding towards my bike. 'You'll be going on that, will you?'

'Probably not, actually,' I replied. 'There's a train you can catch a good part of the way.'

'Is there now? Well, that's handy, isn't it?'

'Yes, I suppose it is.'

He looked at my tent. 'So what brings you to this part of the country then?'

'Well,' I said. 'I've always fancied seeing the lakes, so I thought I'd have a couple of weeks here first.'

'And do you like it so far?'

'What I've seen, yeah.'

'That's good. You going out today?'

'Not sure what I'll be doing really.'

'We've noticed you go out most days.'

'Have you?'

'Yes, we don't miss much from our window.'

I was slightly surprised by this. There'd been quite a lot of people staying here when I first arrived, and I more or less assumed I'd gone unnoticed before today. After all, I was only one tent and a motorbike. Some of the families who'd been around during the week had set up huge encampments that extended across large areas of the field, with countless children running in all directions. By comparison I'd occupied hardly any room at all. Nevertheless, it had taken me some time just to find a reasonable space for myself, where I wouldn't be encroached upon. The previous evening a mass exodus had taken place following a brief spell of rain, but not until this morning did I realize I was the only visitor left. All that remained was an expanse of grass marked out in yellowing squares. The absence of other paying customers probably explained the proprietor's sudden interest in me, yet it turned out he'd been aware of my presence all along.

His remark about the window caused us both to look up at the house, perched on the sloping ground above. Behind it I could make out the outline of a very large barn, as well as some other outbuildings, and beyond them lay the upper slopes of the fells. The whole place was bathed in sunlight, but I knew after yesterday's rain that it wasn't always like this.

As we stood there taking in the view a thought occurred to me.

'What I'd really like to do is hire one of those rowing boats down by the lake.'

'Oh yes?' he said.

'Yeah, but every time I go down there the boat-hire place seems to be closed.'

'Bit late in the season really.'

'Suppose so.'

'Still, I've no doubt you'll find something else to do.'

And with that he gave me a smile and a nod before strolling off in the direction of the house.

'Nice talking to you,' I said to his back, and he raised a hand in acknowledgement.

I watched him go, then delved in my bag for a can of baked beans and set about preparing some breakfast. It was a simple affair, because all I had was a stove, a pan and these beans. I heated them up and ate them 'cowboy-style', without a plate. Then I went over to the tap, washed the pan out and brought back some water for making tea.

While I was waiting for it to boil I sat in the grass and wondered how I was going to occupy myself today. That was the only trouble with this place: the scenery was great and everything, but there was nothing to do except 'take it in', and, to tell the truth, I'd already had enough of that. I'd

ridden round and round the area a few times on my motorbike, going along the edge of lakes and traversing high mountain passes, but there was a limit to how much enjoyment
could be derived from this, especially with all the cars travelling nose to tail everywhere I went. Admittedly the roads
would be quieter now that the majority of tourists had gone
home, yet the idea of spending another day motorcycling
didn't really appeal to me. The alternative, of course, was
going for a walk. There were miles and miles of footpaths
going off in every direction all over the fells, most of them
worn down by sheep, but some, apparently, attributable to
the Romans. I'd read somewhere that you could walk over
the fells for a year and never use the same pathway twice.
Impressive enough, but the disadvantage of going for long
walks was that I'd probably never meet anybody all day long.
So that wasn't particularly attractive either.

However, I was aware that my supply of baked beans was
running low, so I decided to take a short walk along the side
of the lake and get some more. There was a place called
Millfold about a mile away at the northern end, with a shop,
two pubs, a phone box and a churchyard. I'd taken quite a
liking to one of the pubs, the Packhorse, and spent every
evening there, watching people come and go. I had no intention of calling in for a lunchtime drink, though, as I didn't
want the day to dissolve into an alcoholic blur. Once I'd
bought my supplies I would have to think of something else
to do in the afternoon.

I'd made up my mind about that, and was just brewing
the tea, when a movement caught my eye. Walking down
the narrow concrete road that led from the house came a
teenage girl in school uniform. I looked at my watch. It was
eight-thirty. I'd seen this girl go by every day last week,
passing the field full of tents on her way to the front gate.
Here she would stop and stand waiting with a school bag

dangling at her feet. On previous occasions she'd paid no attention to me as she walked past, always looking straight ahead, but this morning she glanced in my direction so I gave her a friendly wave. She waved back and then continued to the gate. The tea now being ready, I poured it into my tin mug and added milk. A few moments later, when I again looked towards the gateway, the schoolgirl had gone. Behind the hedge I could see the roof of a blue minibus moving away along the road.

*   *   *

There was a modest sign fixed to the outside wall of the shower block. 'HILLHOUSE CAMPING', it said. 'PROPRIETOR: T. PARKER'.

After taking a shower I zipped up the tent and set off on my lakeside walk, going out through the main gateway, then across the public road to another gate leading into a second field. Until yesterday this other gate had been wide open and held that way with a chain, giving full access to the lake. It was even open late last night when I came back from the pub. Now, however, the same chain had been used to keep the gate shut, which seemed to indicate that the holiday season was definitely finished. I climbed over and crossed the field by way of a dirt track, passing between some mossy trees before eventually arriving at the lake, where a number of rowing boats were moored. There were seven boats all told, tied up one behind the other, about sixty yards from the shore. As usual the green boat-hire hut was 'closed until further notice', but I went and stood at the end of the small jetty for a while, on the off chance that someone would turn up.

Nobody did, so after a few minutes spent gazing at the water I continued my journey along the shore. Finally, I arrived at the north end of the lake, passed through a kissing gate, and walked across a deserted car park to a sort of square occupied by the shop and the two pubs.

The shopkeeper was standing in his doorway, and appeared to be sunning himself. Above his front window was one large word: 'HODGE'.

'Morning,' he said, as I approached. 'No bike today?'

'Er . . . no,' I replied. 'I thought I'd walk.'

'You're the chap staying up at Tommy Parker's, aren't you?'

'Yes, that's right.'

'Not leaving yet then?'

'No, I thought I'd stay on a bit longer.'

'Oh, I see.'

As I came forward he made a move as if to step back into the shop, but then he paused and remained blocking the doorway instead. As a result I found myself standing quite close to him.

A moment passed as he glanced up at the sky.

'Not a bad sort of day, is it?'

'No, it's very nice,' I agreed, looking up at the same sky.

He seemed content with this answer, and moved aside. Then he followed me into the shop and slipped behind the counter.

'Now then. What can I do you for?'

'Just a few things,' I said. 'Starting with six cans of baked beans.'

'Oh yes,' he said. 'You like your beans, don't you?'

'Yeah, well, they save worrying about meals and everything.'

'Best things ever invented, beans are,' he announced. 'Right then, six cans coming up.'

'Those eggs fresh, are they?' I asked, indicating a box.

'Quite fresh, yes.'

'OK, half a dozen eggs as well, please.'

I bought a carton of milk too, and then paid him.

As he handed over my change he said, 'That motorbike of yours. You thinking of selling it?'

'Not really, no,' I replied.

'I noticed it's quite an early model.'

'Yes,' I said. 'Pre-unit.'

'But it's not for sale?'

'No.'

'Well, if it was, Tommy could sell it for you. Knows all about auctions.'

'Does he?'

'Oh yes. He's always buying and selling things.'

'Oh, right,' I said. 'I'll bear that in mind if I suddenly decide to sell it.'

He gave me a funny look when I said this, but I wasn't bothered really because I thought his questioning was a bit too familiar. After all, I was only a temporary visitor passing though the area, who happened to be buying a few groceries. What did he expect? My life history?

I left the shop and headed across the square. For some reason I'd decided to return to the campsite directly along the public road. There was now a vague notion in my head that I would give the bike a bit of a check-over, and then maybe polish up the chrome. It seemed like a good idea while the nice weather held. Outside the Packhorse a brewer's lorry was making a delivery and collecting a few empty beer barrels. Beside it was one of the barmen, and as I passed by he gave me a nod of recognition.

'How're you doing?' he asked in a cheery manner.

'Alright, thanks,' I replied, and went on my way wondering what sort of lives these people would lead now that the seasonal throng had departed. Despite the sunshine and the chirping birds there was no one else around but me.

I'd just stopped to admire the sheer density and thickness of the churchyard wall, when a pick-up truck with an empty trailer in tow pulled up beside me. Behind the wheel was Mr Parker.

'Want a lift?'

I felt I really ought to decline the offer as it seemed to be my duty to walk on such a pleasant day. But I got in all the same.

'Thanks,' I said, joining him in the cab.

We moved off and then he said, 'Don't mind me asking, but this job of yours you had.'

'Oh, yes?'

'What were you doing?'

'Nothing very special. It was in a factory.'

'Get away.'

'No,' I said. 'Really. It was.'

'What, with chimneys and everything?'

'There was one chimney, yes.'

'But I thought all the factories were supposed to have closed down.'

'Not this one,' I said. 'It was doing quite well actually.'

'Was that down south?'

'Well, south-west really.'

'But you're from the south, aren't you?'

'Er . . . no,' I said. 'Middle, to be exact.'

'Because most of the people who come here are from the north-east.'

'Yes, I've noticed that.'

'Not all of them, of course, but most.'

'Yes.'

It had taken me almost an hour to walk to the shop from the campsite, what with hanging around by the boat-hire place and everything, but in the truck the return journey took only a matter of minutes. We very quickly arrived at Mr Parker's gateway, where he pulled up. Slipping the gears into neutral, he sat tapping his fingers on the steering wheel.

'So what did they make in this factory of yours?' he asked.

'Well, factory's probably the wrong word,' I said. 'It was recycling oil drums. You know, cleaning them out, getting rid of the dents, painting them up.'

'Then they'd sell them off, would they?'

'That's right.'

'And you say they're doing quite well at it?'

'As far as I know, yes.'

'I've got some oil drums up in the top yard. Do you think they'd buy them off me?'

'I'm not sure really,' I said. 'How many have you got?'

'About a dozen,' he replied. 'Picked them up in a job lot.'

'Well, I was only there temporary but I should think you'd need at least a hundred to make it worth while.'

'Oh,' he said. 'I see.'

'Need a full lorry-load really, going all that way.'

'Yes, I suppose it would.' He tapped on the steering wheel again. 'So what job were you doing then?'

'I was in the paint shop.'

'Painting?'

'Well, it was spraying really.'

'Not brushes?'

'No.'

A few moments passed.

'But you can handle a paintbrush, can you?' he asked.

'Not bad with one,' I replied. 'Haven't done much though.'

'Well, we've got a bit of a chore for you if you're interested.'

'Oh,' I said, with some surprise. 'What's that then?'

'This gate needs painting.'

I glanced at the gate that was hooked open beside us. It was a steel tube type, painted red and hinged on substantial concrete posts.

'It's already been painted,' I remarked.

'Wrong colour,' he said. 'It needs to be green.'

'Oh,' I said. 'Well, I can paint it for you if you like.'

'How much would you want for doing that then?'

'I'm not really bothered about the money.'

'Well, you wouldn't want to work for nothing, would you?'

'Tell you what,' I said. 'Let me off the remainder of my rent and that'll do.'

'You sure?'

'Yes, positive. It'll be something to keep me occupied. I quite like painting.'

'Oh, right,' said Mr Parker. 'Well, when you're ready come up to the house and I'll sort you out some paint and suchlike.'

'OK then.'

I got out of the truck and watched as he continued up the concrete road in the direction of his house. As soon as he'd gone it occurred to me that I'd probably diddled myself. What I should have done was charge him a fiver and he'd most likely have let me off the rent anyway. After all, I was hardly taking up any space in his field. Still, it was too late to worry about that now, and to tell the truth I wasn't really bothered. It was actually quite nice to have something proper to do for a change, and so as soon as I'd dumped my groceries in the tent I set off up towards the house.

The camping field was on flat ground, but the concrete road started getting quite steep just after it passed the shower block. It was flanked for some distance by sparse thorn hedges before eventually emerging in a hard gravel yard. As I came up the slope I was aware of the house looming above me, overlooking the yard, the road and the fields below. I passed the lower corner of the building and scuffed some gravel with my boots.

'That was quick, you must be keen,' said Mr Parker.

I looked up and saw him standing on a terrace at the side of the house, at the top of some concrete steps.

'Might as well get on with it,' I replied.

'That's what we like to hear.'

Having arrived in the yard I saw straight away that what I'd taken to be a barn was in fact better described as a corrugated steel shed. It stood opposite the house on a huge concrete platform set into the sloping ground. There were large folding doors at the front, and access to the platform was by means of a concrete loading ramp. Concrete had also been used to create the base for an ancient green petrol pump sited beside the platform. Glancing round, I began to wonder exactly how much concrete had been poured on to this piece of hillside. It seemed to crop up all over the place, like some form of indigenous rock.

Parked next to the steel shed was a Morris van that didn't look as if it had been anywhere for years. Further along there were several stone outbuildings, including a hay-loft, as well as a small bothy, apparently unoccupied. The higher side of the yard was bounded by a dry wall, with a gateway through to another area of hard-standing where I could see a group of second-hand oil drums. This, presumably, was what Mr Parker had referred to earlier as the 'top yard'.

Not that I had much time to examine my surroundings in detail. Within moments of my arrival he'd come down the steps to join me.

'Right,' he said. 'Let's go and have a look in the paint shed.'

He led the way to one of the outbuildings and pushed the door open. Inside, on a series of shelves, were dozens of tins of paint, some pristine and unopened, others not so new. He selected one, handed it to me, and then produced a one-inch brush from another shelf. In doing so he pushed the door open a little further, and the daylight revealed yet more paint stacked at the back of the shed.

'Now then,' he said, turning to me. 'Do you know how to rescal a tin of paint?'

'No,' I said. 'Sorry, I don't.'

'Well, I'm surprised about that. I thought you said you worked in a paint shop.'

'Yeah, but that was spray paint. It all came out of pressure pipes.'

'Ah, well,' he said. 'It's easy enough done. When you've finished painting you put the lid back on nice and tight, and then turn the tin upside down for half a minute.'

'Oh,' I said. 'OK.'

'And when you turn it back the right way up, it's sealed. See?'

'Yep.'

The tin I was holding had never been opened before. I also noticed there was no label.

'How do you know what colour it is?' I asked.

'It's green,' he replied.

'Yeah, but how do you know?'

'I got it in a job lot,' he said. 'All the unlabelled ones are green.'

I looked across the yard at the green petrol pump, and the green-painted doors on the big shed.

'Nice colour,' I remarked.

'Can't stand it myself,' said Mr Parker. 'But I haven't any choice.'

*   *   *

A quarter of an hour later, having walked down to the front gate, got the lid off the tin and given the contents a stir, I began my work. The gateway was quite wide, about sixteen feet across, presumably so that arriving campers wouldn't miss the turning. As a result there was a lot of painting to do. I decided that the best way to go about it was to be methodical, so I would start with the hinges, then do the outer frame of the gate before working my way inwards.

Not long after I'd begun, Mr Parker came by in his truck, again with the trailer in tow. As he passed he slowed down and looked at the job in progress, but said nothing.

The same sort of thing happened every time a vehicle went past on the public road. There wasn't much traffic, but occasionally someone would go by, and they always eased up a little to see who was painting Mr Parker's front gate. I wondered whether I looked like a professional painter. Probably not. A genuine tradesman would more than likely have had a van parked near at hand, with the back doors open and a radio blaring out. He'd be in proper overalls as well, whereas I was clad only in a pair of jeans and a T-shirt. My equipment consisted of no more than a brush and a tin of paint. Obviously an amateur. Someone who'd been roped in to do the job because he had nothing better to do. Nevertheless, I was surprised at the interest my presence seemed to arouse amongst passers-by. There must have been thousands of visitors to the area throughout the summer, and the locals would surely be used to outsiders by now. Yet just because a stranger was painting someone's gate, he immediately came under local scrutiny.

Not that I was bothered by all this. The vehicles that went by were few and far between, and their passing broke the monotony of the job. It was actually taking much longer than I'd expected, and although being outside in the sunshine was quite pleasant, I began to find all the fiddly corners and underneath bits rather tedious. I was just working along one of the diagonals when I heard a clinking noise coming along behind the hedgerow. Glancing round, I saw a pick-up truck go by, loaded with crates full of empty milk bottles. It slowed down as it passed, and a moment later the clinking stopped. There then followed the clunk of a gearbox, and the truck came reversing back up to the gateway.

A man wearing a brown linen coat got out.

'Oh,' he said, looking at the gate. 'Tommy's got you doing this, has he?'

'Yeah,' I replied, without stopping work.

'Well, it probably needed doing then.'

'Yes.'

'You're best painting the outside first and the middle'll look after itself.'

'That's what I'm doing,' I said.

He cocked his head sideways and peered along the gate.

'Yes, you're right,' he said. 'You are.'

At this time I happened to be working with the gate half open and half closed, so that I could get at both sides easily. The man now came round the end of the gate and stood beside me, observing.

'Well,' he said at length. 'You seem to be very handy with a paintbrush.'

'Thanks,' I replied.

'I'll just put this a bit nearer. By the way, is Tommy in?'

'No,' I said. 'He went out earlier.'

'Did he say when he was coming back?'

'No.'

'It's just that there's something I ought to see him about really.'

'Oh yes?'

'Nothing very important, but I've got to see him sometime.'

'OK,' I said. 'Shall I tell him you came?'

'No, I shouldn't bother,' he replied. 'It'll keep.'

'Right.'

He fell silent for a moment, and when I looked up I saw he was gazing across at my tent. I'd been crouched down painting for quite a while now, so I stood upright to give my knees a rest.

'Camping here, are you?' he asked.

'Yes, just for a few days.'

'Do you want milk delivered then?'

'It wouldn't be worth your while, would it?'

'I don't mind delivering to tents.'

'Well, I've been getting milk from the shop actually.'

'What, Hodge?'

'Yes,' I said. 'That's the one.'

'But he only does it in cartons. Mine's in bottles, straight from the dairy.'

'Oh, right. Er . . . the thing is, I won't be here much longer.'

'Oh,' he said. 'I see.'

'Thanks anyway.'

'That's alright. If you change your mind, just let me know.'

'Right.'

'I'd best be off now.'

'OK then. Bye.'

'Bye.'

He went back to his truck, then drove off after giving me a wave, and I resumed my painting. I now had only one short section left to do, so I swung the gate round to leave it hooked in the 'open' position. As I did so it caught the tin and knocked it flat, spilling green paint over the concrete. I cursed and quickly grabbed the tin to put it upright again, then set about trying to transfer as much of the lost contents onto the gate as possible. At the same time I pondered how the accident had happened. All afternoon I'd been very careful about where I put the tin in order to avoid this very thing. Now, despite my efforts, there was paint spread everywhere. Then I recalled the words of the dairyman when he said, 'I'll just put this a bit nearer.' I hadn't really taken any notice of what he was doing, but he must have moved the tin. I was sure he didn't put it where it would get knocked over on purpose, but nonetheless he shouldn't have interfered. I got the gate finished as soon as I could, and then turned my attention to the mess on the ground. There was a bright green splodge more than a yard long across the concrete, and it looked terrible.

I couldn't leave it like that, not right in the middle of Mr Parker's front entrance. So after some consideration I decided to paint it into a square. I marked out the shape with a piece of chalky stone, using one of my tent poles to get a straight line. Then carefully I began filling it in. By the time I'd finished doing this the gate was touch dry. I stood looking at the new green square and wondered if I'd done the right thing or not. Still, it was too late to worry now. After I'd cleaned the paintbrush I went and made a cup of tea. It struck me that I'd not eaten for several hours, so I prepared a pan of beans as well. Finally, I sat down for a rest.

About twenty minutes later the blue minibus I'd seen in the morning drew up outside the front entrance. My watch now said four o'clock. I saw the schoolgirl get out of the vehicle, wave to someone inside as it drove away, and then walk up the concrete road towards the house. This time she took no notice of me at all. After she'd gone I went across to the gate to see if she'd left any footmarks on the green square.

She hadn't.

*   *   *

Night was falling when I saw a pair of headlights come along the public road and turn into the gateway. I could just make out the outline of Mr Parker's pick-up truck and trailer, which seemed to be loaded with something bulky. As the lights flashed up the hill, I got my towel and went over to the shower block. There was an orange-coloured lamp mounted above the men's entrance, and I allowed its dull glow to guide me through the darkness. During the last few days I'd got used to passing between dimly lit tents in which muffled conversations were being held. Tonight, though, there was only me in the entire field, walking silent and barefoot across the grass. I entered the block and was at once dazzled by a powerful fluorescent light set above the wash basins. It shone on the white tiles and the whitewashed walls, making the place seem very stark and bare. When my eyes had become accustomed to the brightness I chose a shower cubicle and turned the tap on. Oddly enough I discovered it was already fully open, but there was no water coming out. I tried the tap in the next cubicle and it was the same. I was just about to test a third one when for some reason all the showers came on together. The water seemed quite warm so I got under one of them straightaway and began applying some soap. It wasn't as steaming hot as it had been on pre- vious occasions, but it would do for a quick splash. Half a minute later, however, the water ran cold so I quickly rinsed the lather off and came out again. I was standing there wondering what had happened when the schoolgirl walked into the shower block carrying a mop.

2

'Have I interrupted?' she asked.

'No, it's OK,' I replied. 'I've just finished.'

'Well, will you be wanting another shower at all?'

'Er . . . not today, no. Thanks.'

'What about tomorrow?'

'Oh yes, I'd like one in the morning.'

'It's just that we'll be turning the water off at nights now.'

'Why's that then?'

'In case there's a sudden frost.'

'It gets that cold, does it?'

'It might do,' she said. 'And there's a lot of exposed piping.'

'Oh,' I said. 'Well, what will I do about a shower?'

'I'll have to show you how to turn it on and off.'

All the showers were still going at full force as we were talking, so we had to raise our voices a little to make ourselves heard. I stood with the towel wrapped around my waist while this young girl explained the plumbing system.

She started by pointing into the cubicle. 'All you do is leave the shower taps turned fully on. You needn't touch them at all. Then if you'll just follow me.' She led the way out of the men's block, through the darkness outside and back into the empty ladies' section. The layout here was just the same as in the men's, except that there were more mirrors. All the ladies' showers were going at full belt as well.

'This big tap here is the stopcock for the main supply,' she continued. 'So you open it up before you have your shower and shut it off after.'

'Open before and shut after,' I repeated. 'Right.'

'And the other red tap down the bottom is for draining the entire system out. So you close it first, and open it after.'

'Isn't all this a bit of a waste of water?' I asked.

'Not really,' she replied. 'There's plenty more where that came from.'

'Oh, OK,' I said.

'Have you got all that then?'

'Yes, thanks.'

'Good.'

She started to head back towards the men's block.

'And you are?' I enquired.

'Gail Parker.'

'So you're Mr Parker's daughter, are you?'

'That's right.'

'Oh well, thanks again for your help. Bye.'

'Bye.'

And she was gone. I stood outside the men's block listening for a few moments as she began swishing the showers with her mop, and then I went back to the tent to get dressed. After that there was nothing to do except go down the pub. I had a choice between walking or going on the bike. If I took the bike it meant I would have to drink less, maximum three pints. Or I could walk and have five. I thought of the money I'd saved by painting Mr Parker's gate, and decided to walk.

Half an hour later I arrived at the 'bottom bar' of the Packhorse. There were two entrances. One was through the front door, past the pay-phone and down a carpeted hallway. The other one, which I preferred, was by a side door from the beer garden. On the door was a notice: 'DARTS IN PROGRESS', it said. 'KNOCK BEFORE ENTERING'.

I ignored this and pushed open the door.

'Wait a sec!' said an urgent voice within.

I stopped and waited. There followed the sound of three gentle thuds.

'Alright,' said the voice. 'You can come in now.'

I entered and was greeted by the barman I'd seen earlier in the day. He was withdrawing three darts from a board in the corner behind the door. Glancing round I saw that I was the only customer.

'No one uses that door in the winter,' he said with a friendly smile. 'You'd be better off coming round by the top bar.'

'Oh, right,' I said. 'Sorry, I'll do that in future.'

I'd seen the warning notice before, of course, but never really taken it seriously. After all, I'd come through the same doorway every night up to now, and there'd been no obvious risk of being impaled by a dart. In fact, there hadn't even been a dartboard: just an empty wooden frame full of tiny holes. Above this was a shaded metal lamp, and at one side a black scoring margin with the words 'HOME' and 'AWAY' in stencilled gold lettering. Until tonight, however, the dartboard itself had remained absent. Now it was back in use, and the door to the beer garden was not recommended.

'I'll have to lock that,' said the barman. 'Don't want any accidents, do we?'

'No, I suppose not,' I replied. 'Does that mean the beer garden's out of bounds now?'

'Well, it's only there for the tourists really,' he said. 'And they've all gone.'

'Except me.'

'You don't count.'

'Don't I?'

'Not if you're still here at this time of year, no,' he said. 'Pint of Ex?'

By now he'd gone behind the counter, and had in fact already begun working the hand pump before asking what I wanted.

'Yes, please,' I said.

'You'll have to make the most of it,' he announced. 'This is the last barrel. It'll be gone in a few days.'

'That's alright by me,' I remarked. 'I'm only here 'til the end of the week.'

'Oh well,' he said. 'You can help see it off then, can't you?'

He placed a perfect pint of Topham's Excelsior Bitter on the counter, and I paid him.

'Won't you be getting any more after that?' I asked.

'We'd never sell enough to make it worth while,' he replied.

'What about the locals though? Don't they drink it?'

'Course not,' he said with a grin. 'They're not interested in real ale.'

'Aren't they?'

'No, they much prefer keg beers. Lager and suchlike. You know, from a factory.'

He came back from behind the counter and resumed his darts practice. A moment later he turned to me again with a puzzled look on his face.

'Did you say you were leaving at the end of the week?'

'That's the plan,' I said.

'But I thought you were doing the painting along there at Hillhouse?'

'Oh,' I said. 'You know about that then, do you?'

'Gordon said he saw you doing the front gate this afternoon. Said you were talking to Deakin.'

I knew Gordon was the other barman at the Packhorse. I'd seen him working alongside my present host during previous visits, and had heard his name spoken a couple of times. However, I had no idea who Deakin was.

'Who's Deakin?' I asked.

'You know Deakin,' he said. 'Fellow who does the milk round.'

'Oh, him,' I said. 'Yes, well, I wasn't talking to him really. He was talking to me.'

'That sounds like Deakin alright.'

'But I was only doing the one gate,' I added. 'Just helping out, you know.'

'So you're not staying on then?'

'Not for long, no.'

'Oh,' he said. 'I see. Play darts, do you?'

'Now and then, yes.'

'Want a game?'

'Well, it's a while since I've thrown a dart in anger.'

'That's alright,' he said. 'It'll help pass the time. Got your own arrows?'

'Er . . . no.'

'Right,' he said. 'You use these and I'll get another set.'

He produced some more darts from behind the counter, and we had a game of 301, which he won. When he chalked up the score he put himself down as 'T', and I then remembered I'd heard someone call him Tony the night before. Another game followed, which he won again. It seemed that despite the recent absence of a dartboard he'd not fallen out of practice, and once he was onto a double the match would be a foregone conclusion. In the third game, however, I managed to keep up with him, and he didn't defeat me quite so easily.

'Shot,' I said, as he landed the required double eight to win.

'Thanks,' he replied. 'You throw a nice dart yourself.'

'Thanks.'

'Best of seven?'

'Might as well.'

'Tony!' called a voice at the other end of the pub.

'Back in a sec.'

He slipped behind the counter and went to serve a new-comer up in the 'top bar'. 'Now then, Bryan,' I heard him say.

I hadn't been in the other part of the pub, but I knew that it was always referred to as the 'top bar'. I had the feeling that it was reserved for the locals, whereas tourists were expected to the use the 'bottom bar'. For some reason the Packhorse had been built on two levels, and although both halves were joined together the top bar was two steps higher up with its own separate counter and beer pumps. As a result, the people who drank there had a slightly superior and exclusive look about them, when seen from below. The top bar was usually presided over by an older man whom I took to be the landlord, while Tony and Gordon looked after the much busier bottom bar. Tonight, however, things were very quiet and Tony appeared to be running the whole place on his own. As I waited for our darts game to continue, I glanced through at the new customer in the other bar. Yes, I thought, definitely a local, and I knew I'd seen him before because I recognized his cardboard crown. It was silver with three points, and had been repaired at some time or other with Sellotape. I'd noticed this man quite often up in the top bar, and on each occasion he'd had the cardboard crown on his head. When he caught my gaze he grinned and nodded in my direction, saying something to Tony. I couldn't hear what it was, but it didn't seem unfriendly.

A few moments later Tony returned to the dartboard and play began again. It was best of seven, which he won four games to one, so we made it best of nine and he won that as well. Still, as he'd rightly said, it did help pass the time. During the evening a few other customers arrived at the Packhorse, and without exception they turned out to be locals. Most of them headed for the top bar, but one or two came down our end. As they drifted in they gave the impression that it was their first visit to the bottom bar for some time. It was almost as if they were reclaiming lost territory.

'Peace and quiet at last,' said one man as he walked in, and immediately moved a bar stool so that he could sit with his back to the corner wall. This reminded me of an incident I'd witnessed the previous week when a customer had carted a stool from one end of the bar to the other. The landlord had been on him immediately, ordering him to leave the 'furniture' where it was, and if he didn't like it he could take his custom somewhere else. The hapless victim had been with a large group of others, all tourists by the look of them, and shortly afterwards the whole lot had drunk up and left. Somehow I couldn't picture a similar episode taking place with any of the present crowd. The rules were different now that the tourist season was over. Locals, it seemed, were free to move the stools wherever they pleased. Nevertheless, at the time this treatment of a paying customer had struck me as quite rude. I suspected that Tony was the landlord's son, since there was a noticeable resemblance between the two, but fortunately the similarity ended there. Tony couldn't have been more pleasant, and even though I was technically a 'tourist', he'd gone out of his way to make me feel welcome. The same applied to Gordon. Both junior barmen appeared to be roughly the same age as me, and I felt an affinity with the pair of them. I was unable to tell, however, whether they were permanently attached to the Packhorse. They each seemed the type who would probably have been expected to do something 'better' than just work in a pub, and I liked to imagine they were only doing this until something else turned up. The idea of just staying here for ever, and never moving on, seemed quite unthinkable.

After a while the two bars became busy enough to keep Tony fully occupied, so he was forced to abandon the darts. Other players came forward, though, and I had several more games, and even won a few. Shortly we were joined in the bottom bar by the man in the cardboard crown. He'd obviously come down for a game of darts, because he went and added a 'B' to the list of people waiting to play. The local rule was winner-stays-on, and there were two initials ahead of his, so in the meantime he went and talked to the man who'd moved the bar stool.

I wasn't really taking much notice, but I thought they nodded towards me a couple of times during their conversation. A moment later the one with the crown addressed me directly.

'Was that you who painted the green square up at Tommy Parker's?' he asked.

'Well, sort of,' I answered. 'But it wasn't entirely my fault.'

They were both grinning at me, and I suddenly became aware that the other customers standing round the bar were all listening to the exchange.

'Whose fault was it then?'

Not wishing to incriminate anyone I said, 'It was just an accident, that's all.'

'You mean you accidentally painted a green square?'

This caused several people to laugh out loud.

'No,' I said. 'But that's how it ended up.'

'Well, Tommy's not going to be best pleased about it.'

'Isn't he?'

'No, he is not.'

The laughter faded away.

'I suppose you won't have seen him lose his temper yet?' said someone over by the dartboard.

'Er . . . no,' I replied. 'I haven't, no.'

I must have started to look quite alarmed because the man

in the crown suddenly stepped forward and slapped me on the back.

'Don't you worry about it, lad,' he said. 'It's not the end of the world. Come on, we'll buy you a drink.'

Next thing there was a full pint of beer in my hand, paid for by the man in the cardboard crown. The rest of the evening passed in a haze of beer drinking and darts playing. I ended up buying him two pints back for the one he'd bought me, but as I told myself later, it was the thought that counted. When last orders finally came I decided I'd had enough drink for one night, and left them all buying further rounds for each other. Ten minutes later I was wandering along the side of the lake, tripping over tree roots as I tried to follow the footpath in the dark.

It was the drink, I suppose, that made me decide to come this way instead of going along the road. Just as it was the drink that impelled me on to the jetty when I got to the boat-hire place. I went and stood at the very end, from where I could just make out the seven rowing boats lined up on their mooring. There was another road running along the far side of the lake, and while I was standing there I noticed a vehicle's lights coming up from the south. It was over half a mile away, but even from that distance it struck me as being very brightly lit. As well as the headlights I could see a number of glowing shapes on the roof, but I was unable to make out what they were. The vehicle disappeared for a moment or two as it passed amongst some trees, and then emerged again further along the lakeside. By now it was almost opposite to where I stood. A slight breeze had got up during the evening, and this carried the noise of a whirring engine, and the rumble of tyres on the distant road surface.

And then another sound drifted across the lake. It only lasted for a few seconds and I couldn't tell where it came from, yet it seemed vaguely familiar. A remote melody was being chimed out in the darkness, and I recognized a small segment from a nursery rhyme. The part that went 'Half a pound of treacle'. Then it had gone again, and all that remained was the sound of the trees gently stirring, and the lake lapping against the shore.

*   *   *

I had a headache when I woke up next morning. It had been my intention to take a drink of water from the standpipe before I went to bed, but by the time I got back to the campsite I'd forgotten all about it. Instead I'd crawled into my tent and gone straight to sleep, and now I had a hangover. This was the price for drinking five pints of Topham's Excelsior Bitter. Or was it six? I couldn't recollect clearly, but I decided that a quick shower would clear away the fuzziness. As I approached the shower block I remembered about having to turn the supply on, so I discreetly entered the ladies' and went through the routine the schoolgirl had shown me. It all seemed to work OK, but when I went round to the men's block I found the water was running completely cold. I then realized that the few moments of warm water I'd enjoyed the previous evening must have been the last drops of the heated supply. From now on, if I wanted a shower, it was going to be cold water only. This struck me as a bit of a swizz. After all, if someone paid rent to stay at a campsite, they should surely be entitled to some hot water. Then it occurred to me that I hadn't actually paid any rent for this week. I'd painted a gate instead. Therefore I had no choice but to brace myself for a thirty-second cold shower. I stepped under the nozzle and stood naked and shivering in the icy deluge.

Which was when I recalled the man in the cardboard crown, and his questions about the green square. Had he really interrogated me in front of the entire pub? Yes, he had. They'd all stood round listening, and then someone had asked if I'd seen Mr Parker lose his temper yet. Obviously, of course, I hadn't. I'd only been here a few days and had barely set eyes on him. Yet they'd all behaved as though the matter was of great importance. Well, personally I couldn't see what all the fuss was about. Alright, so I accepted that Mr Parker wouldn't be delighted by the sight of a green-painted square in the middle of his gateway. This was fair enough, but I could hardly imagine him losing his temper over it. On the contrary, he seemed to be the sort of man who took such things in his stride. He'd been nothing but polite and courteous in his dealings with me so far, and I had no doubt that he would remain the same despite this episode with the spilt paint.

When I'd got dressed I went round to turn the water off, and then headed back to my tent. On the way I noticed Mr Parker standing by the gate, opening and closing it and giving the paintwork a thorough examination. I decided I might as well go across straight away and make sure he was satisfied with my efforts, so I casually strolled over. As I approached and joined him he gave me a brief glance, but then continued gazing at the gate in a preoccupied way. He appeared to pay no attention to the green square under his feet, or to the person who painted it. Instead he just stood there in silence. Not until several long moments had gone by did he turn and speak at last.

'Did you say you wanted to take a boat out?'

'Er . . . yes,' I said. 'I would quite like to.'

'Well, you can if you wish.'

'Oh, right. You can fix it up, can you?'

He smiled. 'I can fix anything up.'

'So are they your boats?'

'I have the main interest in them, yes.'

'Oh,' I said. 'I never realized that.'

'Do you want to go this morning?'

'Yeah, that'd be great.'

'Alright, well, I'll come by in about half an hour and we'll go and sort you one out.'

'OK,' I said. 'Thanks.'

After he'd gone I looked again at the green square and wondered why the men in the pub had made such a big deal about it. After all, Mr Parker hadn't even mentioned the subject. Admittedly the square was very difficult to ignore, especially in the broad light of a new day, but I soon came to the conclusion that they were trying to create something out of nothing because they had little else to talk about. I decided to put the whole thing out of my mind and instead make the most of this morning's generous offer.

Mr Parker came back in his pick-up shortly after I'd finished my breakfast of baked beans and a mug of tea.

'Very sparse existence you've got here,' he remarked as I joined him in the cab.

'Well, it's only for a few days,' I said. 'Makes a nice change, really.'

'You like hardship then, do you?'

'Not particularly, but as I say, it's only a few days.'

'And then you'll be off on your travels?'

'That's the plan, yes.'

As we talked we had been slowly trundling towards the entrance to the lower field, where we now arrived.

'Unlock the gate, will you?' said Mr Parker.

He handed me a key and I got out and unchained the gate. It was another sunny day, and as we continued in the direction of the lake I felt quite privileged to have the whole place to myself. Mr Parker drove at a leisurely pace, and appeared to be inspecting the property as we passed through it. At the far side of the field he paused to look at some fallen branches scattered amongst the mossy trees. Also to examine the broken remains of an upturned boat lying beside the dirt track. I'd seen this boat each time I went by on the way to the pub, and guessed it had lain abandoned for many years. There were several species of plants and small trees growing through the bottom where the wood had rotted, and to my eyes it made quite an attractive landmark.

'We'll have to get rid of that sometime,' announced Mr Parker.

'Don't you like it then?' I asked.

'No, I do not,' he said. 'Most unsightly.'

'I think it looks quite nice myself,' I remarked. 'Very rustic.'

He shook his head. 'It's no good it being rustic if it's no use.'

'Oh, well, no,' I said carefully. 'No, I suppose not.'

We carried on to the lake, and pulled up beside the green boat-hire hut. Mr Parker produced another key and after a couple of tries unlocked the door. As it opened there was a cracking of new paint, and I realized that the hut had been given its coat of green quite recently.

'Someone's been busy,' I said.

'Yes,' he replied. 'We like to keep on top of the painting.'

'I've noticed that.'

To tell the truth, whoever painted it hadn't done a very good job. There were runs everywhere and the door seemed to have been shut before the paint was even dry. Definitely not a piece of professional workmanship. However, I made no comment on the matter, and waited while Mr Parker peered into the hut, as if trying to get accustomed to the gloom within.

'By the way,' he continued. 'Have you done any rowing before?'

'Well, not since I was a child,' I said. 'We used to live near a park with a boating pond.'

'So you can row, can you?'

'Yeah, it's like riding a bike.'

'I mean to say, we wouldn't want you getting into any difficulties.'

'No, I'll be OK. Thanks.'

'You won't need rescuing after ten minutes then?'

'I doubt it.'

'Very good.' He turned and faced me in the doorway. 'Right, that'll be one pound for the hire of a boat please.'

'Oh,' I said. 'Sorry, I didn't realize . . .'

He glanced at the lake and then back at me. 'Something wrong?'

'Er . . . no, it's alright. Have you got any change?'

'Not on me, no.'

'The thing is, I've only got notes. Sorry.'

'Oh,' he said. 'I see.'

'Can I owe it you for the time being?'

He considered this for a moment, peering into the hut again.

'I suppose you can, yes,' he said at length. 'For the time being.'

'Thanks.'

'Now then, while we're both here we'll just see if we can get this open.'

He disappeared inside, and I could hear him unfastening some bolts behind a hatchway in the front of the hut. It sounded like he was having a bit of a struggle, so I tried to see what I could do to help from the outside. The hatch was about four feet long and looked as if it was supposed to open outwards. Unfortunately, the paint seemed to be sticking, so I began prodding and poking at various points. As I did so, Mr Parker continued speaking in a muffled tone from inside the hut.

'I've never taken to boating myself.'

'Haven't you?' I said, raising my voice a little so he could hear me.

'No,' he replied. 'I've tried it, but I didn't like it.'

'That's a shame. Maybe you should give it another go.'

'I haven't time to go playing around in boats.'

'Oh. No. I don't imagine you have.'

'Got more important things to do.'

'Yeah.'

'So today I'll be leaving you to your own devices, if that's alright.'

'OK.'

The bottom of the hatch moved slightly in my direction. There was a small gap underneath, so I stuck my fingers in to try and help pull. A moment later a sharp rattling noise came from inside the hut. The right-hand corner of the hatch was now free, but the left corner remained stuck.

'Are you pushing or pulling?' asked Mr Parker.

'Er . . . pulling, actually,' I replied.

'Well, can you pull a bit harder? Please?'

We were now both speaking with raised voices. I gripped and pulled. At the same time I heard a grunt from inside, and the hatch quickly opened outwards, jamming my knuckles for a moment before swinging up at me. I stepped back and let go, allowing the hatch to slam shut again.

'Flaming hell!' roared a voice within. 'Keep hold of it then!'

'Sorry,' I said, attempting to get my fingers back under. This hurt somewhat, as my knuckles had been grazed quite badly. Next instant the hatch swung up again to reveal Mr Parker doing battle with a wooden support prop, which he instantly began jamming into position. I noticed his face had turned a deep pink and his eyes were blazing. It seemed important that this part of the operation should be completed as quickly as possible, so I grabbed the prop and helped guide it with my free hand, while still holding on to the hatch with the other. A few seconds later the prop was safely in place, and the struggle was over. There then followed a brief silence. I didn't say anything to Mr Parker, but instead pretended to gaze out across the lake in a preoccupied manner.

When he spoke again his tone of voice had returned to normal.

'We'll have to have a look at this hatch sometime,' he remarked. 'Seems to be sticking at one side.'

'Yes,' I agreed, casting an expert eye over the hatchway. 'Must be the new paint.'

'Or perhaps a bit of sagging in the timber.'

'Could be, I suppose.'

'Right, then. Can you give me a hand with the tender please?'

Leaning against the back wall of the hut I could see a tiny boat, no more than five feet long. By the time I got inside he'd already begun struggling to lift it, so I quickly grabbed the other end. We lugged it out of the hut and across to the water's edge, our legs moving in short little jerks like a beetle. After a moment's rest we continued along the jetty. In so doing I became increasingly aware that the structure wasn't in particularly sound condition. It was alright for normal walking about on, but under the additional weight of the boat a few planks creaked and made other ominous noises. Finally, however, we got to the end, where we put the boat down. Mr Parker then walked back along the jetty, giving it an inspection as he went. I could see that several planks were cracked and insecure, while others showed early signs of rot. There were even one or two missing altogether.

'Needs a bit of maintenance here,' he remarked. 'Do you want to come and get some oars?'

'Oh yeah,' I said. 'Forgot about them.'

I followed him back to the hut, where he handed me the oars before locking up.

'Pull the tender in among those reeds when you've finished,' he said. 'Should be safe there for the time being.'

'OK.'

'Right, then. I'll leave you to it.'

'How long shall I stay out for?' I asked.

'As long as you like,' replied Mr Parker. 'There's no one else here.'

After he'd gone I went back to the end of the jetty and launched the tender. Then I stood looking at it, wondering what to do next. I'd assumed that he meant me to use it to get to the full-sized rowing boats out on the mooring, but I wasn't entirely certain about this. Maybe I was just supposed to potter around in this tiny thing for a couple of hours, and then come back. After all, he'd never actually mentioned the other boats while he was here. And I hadn't liked to ask. So now I found myself in a bit of a quandary.

Yet surely on a lake this size someone would need to be in a proper boat to make it worth while. Wouldn't they? Yes, I decided, of course they would. Especially if they were paying a pound for the privilege. With this in mind I set off towards the mooring. I was pleased to find that I hadn't forgotten how to row, and once I'd got used to the balance I was soon well on my way.

As I approached the line of moored boats I began to realize that they bore a strong resemblance to the ones in my childhood park. They were all an identical shade of maroon, and even the gold paintwork along the gunwales looked the same. Most striking of all, though, were the ornate prows that rose up at the front of each boat. As a child I'd always been impressed by these because they reminded me of the curved ships from famous legends and fables. For some reason the raised prows made the boats seem ancient, so that it was impossible to tell whether they were constructed ten, twenty or even fifty years before. It was this sense of age-lessness that had always attracted me to them.

Not that I planned to have an 'adventure' in one of these vessels. After all, I was fully aware that they were just simple pleasure craft, built to be hired out by the hour. I was going for nothing more than a simple jaunt on the lake, enjoying the sunshine whilst taking in the scenery from a new per-spective. Nevertheless, by the time I'd chosen a boat and clambered aboard, the thought had been planted in my head that I didn't just want to spend the morning aimlessly rowing about. It would be much better actually to go on a journey somewhere. Not long after that I hit on the idea of making my way towards the end of the lake, and then having a pint of beer in the Packhorse.

From out here on the water I was made aware of the vastness of the surrounding fells. Silent except for the bleat-ing of distant sheep, they looked as though they went on for ever, although in reality of course I knew they didn't. Less than ten miles to the east a modern motorway cut a swathe right through them. Along this strip of tarmac pounded an endless stream of traffic in the headlong charge between England and Scotland. There was also a railway line, and a procession of electricity pylons carrying power from one industrial centre to another.

Yet from my boat I could seen no evidence of any of this. There was just empty land, and trees, with occasional farms and dwellings scattered along the lakeside. What caught my eye most of all was Mr Parker's house perched high up on the slope. With the huge shed looming in the background, it seemed to dominate the locality, giving the impression that there was someone inside keeping watch. I was sure he had better things to do than spy on me from his window all day, but all the same I felt more at ease when I'd rowed half a mile and the house finally disappeared behind a spur of land.

The boat was moving along quite nicely, and I had to admit that this was a very pleasant way to pass the time. Unfortunately my back had begun complaining about the unaccustomed strain it was under, so I was glad to see the end of the lake drawing near. I knew from my previous walks to the pub that there was a good place to go ashore not far from the car park. I managed to pull the boat on land without getting my feet wet, and as a precaution I tied the mooring rope to a nearby sapling. Then I set off on foot towards the Packhorse.

As I approached I saw that Tony was at work in the beer garden, applying black paint to the outside windowsills of the pub. The walls were whitewashed, with some black beams across the middle, and I assumed that this was meant to make the building appear to be 'Tudor' in origin.

'Doing a good job there,' I said, walking towards the side door. 'Safe to go in, is it?'

'Should be,' he replied. 'But knock first, just in case.'

I knocked and entered the bottom bar, which was deserted. A moment later Tony came in, served me a pint of Ex and then went out again. It was too nice a day to remain inside for very long, so I followed him out into the beer garden where he resumed his painting. I had planned to sit at one of the wooden picnic tables, but I discovered they'd all been treated with wood preserver and stacked one on top of the other in the corner. For this reason I went and sat on the stone wall instead, placing my beer beside me while I waited for it to settle. Occasionally I glanced across the square, but there seemed to be no one about. The only sign of activity this morning was Tony at work with his brush, applying new black paint over the black paint that was already there. A few minutes passed as he completed yet another window-sill. Then I heard a vehicle coming down the road from the direction of the church, and casually looked round to see Mr Parker go by in his pick-up with the trailer in tow.

Suddenly this trip to the Packhorse didn't seem such a good idea. I'd hardly touched my pint before his unexpected appearance, but now I felt the urge to finish it and get back to where I'd tied up. After all, I was supposed to be out on the lake, not lounging in a pub garden. I wasn't sure whether he'd noticed me sitting there, but I was certain he wouldn't be very pleased about one of his boats being left unattended. I drained my glass and headed across the square. As I did so it occurred to me that even at this moment there might be someone making off with the boat. I broke into a run, charging through the deserted car park and up the path to the lake. It was difficult running with the newly swallowed beer inside me, and by the time I got to the water's edge I felt quite sick. The boat was lying exactly where I'd left it, of course, completely safe. As I collapsed out of breath in the grass nearby I realized I'd panicked over nothing, and all because of that conversation last night in the pub. It had been the thought of Mr Parker losing his temper that'd brought me rushing back instead of taking the time to enjoy my beer properly. This now struck me as ridiculous. The episode at the boat-hire hut with the sticking hatch had shown me, if anything, that he controlled his temper very well. I soon came to the conclusion that the whole thing was some sort of local myth, not to be taken seriously.

Still, now I was here I could see no point in going back to the pub for another pint, so once I'd recovered sufficiently I relaunched the boat and continued my rowing. I suppose I must have passed the time in this manner for another hour or so before the novelty wore off. By then I'd worked my way right along the far shore of the lake to a point more or less opposite Mr Parker's place. I decided that this was enough for one day, so I returned to the mooring, tied up and rowed ashore in the tender. I shoved it into the reeds as he'd directed, leaving the oars tucked under the seat. This time I did get my feet wet. The water looked shallow but there was a lot of mud, and my boots sank in while I was getting out of the boat. Despite this it had been an enjoyable couple of hours. I strolled back to the tent, changed my socks and had a cup of tea. My motorbike had been waiting there neglected for a couple of days, so I spent the afternoon giving it the clean I'd promised yesterday.

When I went to the pub that night it struck me that there was a distinct shortage of women in the area now that the tourists had left. The previous week the place had been full of attractive girls, all looking especially healthy after a few days in the outdoors. Now they seemed to have gone. The only exception was a young woman who appeared up in the top bar at about ten o'clock. I'd seen her once before. On that occasion she spent a lot of time talking to Tony, and I'd more or less assumed she was his girlfriend. Tonight, however, Gordon was on duty and she seemed to be giving him the same amount of attention. Which made me think she could be unattached. I quite liked the look of her, and would probably have tried to get acquainted if I hadn't been leaving at the end of the week. As it was, I had to content myself with the occasional glance she gave in my direction.

Meanwhile, in the bottom bar, the dartboard remained the centre of attention. The supply of Topham's Excelsior Bitter seemed to be holding out alright, and I spent another evening with the locals. One darts game followed another, followed by a further round of drinks and another one after that. I wondered if it was like this every night during the winter. They set a very fast pace for their drinking and once again I seemed to get swept along with it. As usual the man in the cardboard crown was present, and he made sure I didn't miss out. I stayed as long as possible to see if the young woman in the top bar left with anybody, but she suddenly dis-appeared while my back was turned. It was time to leave, so I wandered back to the campsite and went straight to bed.

I didn't sleep well. In the middle of the night a girl in a gym slip kept turning the water on and off. I came slowly awake and realized someone was shaking my tent pole.

A moment later I heard a voice outside. It was Mr Parker.

'Could you give us a hand here?' he said. 'The rowing boats seem to have got away.'

3

I could hear an engine running in the darkness.

'Just a sec,' I said, searching for my boots and pulling them on quickly.

When I came out I saw the pick-up truck parked nearby, headlights blazing. Mr Parker had already returned to the driving seat, so I went over and he spoke through the window.

'I've just been down to the lake and there's no sign of them. We'll have to conduct a search.'

I got in beside him and we headed off towards the lower field, where the gate was unchained and wide open. Shortly afterwards we arrived at the water's edge. With some relief I found the tender amongst the reeds where I'd left it. I could just make out its dark shape in the moonlight. The string of boats on the mooring, however, had gone.

'Could you row out and have a look for them?' said Mr Parker.

'Er . . . yeah,' I replied. 'Can if you like.'

This didn't sound like a very good idea to me. After all, the chance of finding seven boats on a lake this size, in the dark, seemed quite small. However, I wanted to appear to be helping in any way I could, so I went along with it. I got my feet wet again as I cast off, but this didn't seem very important under the circumstances. As I rowed slowly away from the shore I could see Mr Parker's figure standing on the jetty, looking in my direction. I got to where the mooring buoy should have been and noticed that it, too, had vanished.

'Can you see them?' called Mr Parker.

'Afraid not,' I called back. 'Looks like the whole mooring's gone.'

'Well, could you search further out?'

This whole exercise was beginning to seem very pointless, as I could hardly see where I was going, let alone catch a glimpse of the escaped boats. To make it worse, the water sounded much noisier tonight that it had done during the day. I could hear it bashing against the tender, and I began to wonder how far it would be safe to go. Still, I carried on plodding along for the time being, in order to satisfy Mr Parker that I'd had a good look. As I did so I wondered what he'd been doing down here at this time of night to notice that the boats had gone. I had no idea what time it was, but it must have been well into the small hours. After a while he called me again.

'Can you come in now, please?'

His way of giving orders in the form of a polite request was very effective, and I suddenly realized I'd inadvertently become his servant. Here I was floating about in the darkness at his beck and call, with wet feet, when I should have been fast asleep. I wasn't unduly bothered about the inconvenience, but all the same I was pleased that he'd at last decided to abandon our search. Now I could go back to bed.

So it was a bit disappointing when I came ashore and he said, 'We'll have to drive round the lake road and see where they've gone.'

'Wouldn't it be better to wait until morning?' I asked.

'Might be too late by then,' he replied. 'And I should hate to lose them.'

We got in the pick-up truck and spent the next two hours on a fruitless search. We went first to Millfold, then over the stone bridge and onto the road that ran south along the far side of the lake. Every time we passed anywhere near the shore Mr Parker stopped and I had to jump out and stand at the water's edge peering into the gloom.

Then I'd get back in and he'd say, 'No sign of them?'

'Sorry, no,' I'd reply, and we'd press on.

There was little other conversation. Occasionally we would pass some property and he'd slow down and look in through the gateway, as if expecting to see his boats hidden somewhere within. Finally, we came to the southernmost tip of the lake and he turned back. I thought that would be enough charging about for one night, but when we arrived at the campsite Mr Parker drove down to the jetty again. For a moment I thought he was hoping the boats had come home of their own accord. Instead it seemed that he'd decided to put the tender back in the hut for safekeeping, so we spent another few minutes struggling to get it locked away. Only then did we rest. Mr Parker had certainly taken the loss of his boats seriously, but there didn't seem to be any suggestion that it was my fault. As far as I could make out the whole mooring must have come adrift from the bed of the lake, and obviously that had nothing to do with me. All the same, I couldn't help wondering if I was somehow 'suspected'.

For his part, Mr Parker was being quite friendly. After he'd locked the hut he turned to me and said, 'You'd better come up to the house for some breakfast.'

By this time several streaks of light had appeared in the eastern sky, so I guessed it was about six o'clock. I was ready for bed, but a bit of breakfast in a proper kitchen sounded very attractive, so I accepted the offer.

When we pulled up in the yard I saw Mr Parker's trailer parked by the big shed. It was loaded with a large piece of equipment whose purpose I couldn't make out in this light.

I was about to ask what it was when the terrace door opened and Gail Parker appeared.

'Found them?' she asked, with some concern in her voice.

'No, we haven't,' replied her father. 'We'll have to have another look when it's light enough. Could you rustle up some breakfast for this one?'

'Morning,' I said, with a polite smile, and she smiled back.

'Eggs and coffee be alright?' she asked.

'Yes, fine, thanks.'

I followed the two of them inside to a warm kitchen with a large wooden table. I noticed Mr Parker left his boots on, so I did the same. Then we sat down and I was given breakfast. This was the first time I'd eaten at a table for some while, and I made the most of it, accepting the eggs and coffee with good grace. There wasn't much talk, but after a while Mr Parker started up a conversation.

'I see your motorbike's quite an early model,' he remarked.

'Yes,' I replied. 'Pre-unit.'

'Had it long?'

'A couple of years, yes.'

'You've hardly been out on it the last few days.'

'No,' I said. 'Suppose I haven't.'

'Been too busy with other things.'

'Yes.'

'You can put it in one of the sheds up here if you like.'

'Oh ... er ... can I?'

'If you like, yes. Then we can keep an eye on it for you.'

'Well thanks anyway, but I'll be going at the end of the week. Hardly seems worth your trouble.'

'Alright, well, if you change your mind.'

'Thanks.'

He glanced out of the window. 'Here's Deakin.'

For the last few moments I'd been aware of a rattling noise

coming up the hill, and next thing a pick-up truck pulled into the yard. Looking out I saw the dairyman leave the vehicle, grab a pint of milk and run up the steps. There was a 'clunk' outside the door, and then he was running back down again. After he'd gone I recalled the conversation I'd had with him while painting the gate, about how he needed to 'see Tommy about something'. I concluded that the matter can't have been as important as he'd made out.

'Met Deakin, have you?' asked Mr Parker.

'Er . . . just once,' I replied. 'Does he come up here every day?'

'Most days, yes.'

'Oh,' I said. 'I didn't know that.'

'Well, you're not usually up this early, are you?'

'No, I suppose not.'

'You're probably still asleep when he goes by.'

At that moment another vehicle pulled up in the yard. This time it was a Post Office van. The driver bobbed up the steps, opened the kitchen door by four inches and slipped the post onto a shelf inside.

'Thank you,' he said, in a sing-song voice, and was gone again in a flash.

'I never realized it got so busy here,' I remarked.

'Yes, there's always something going on,' said Mr Parker.

'Must be nice having your own postman.'

'Don't people have their own postmen in the south then?'

'Well, yeah, but they don't usually have their own van as well.'

'Oh, that's right,' he said. 'They all go around on bicycles, don't they? With big sacks.'

'Some of them do, yes,' I replied. 'But it's more sort of house-to-house.'

At that moment a telephone rang in the adjoining room, instantly causing Gail to spring from her seat.

'I'll get it,' she said, darting next door.

A moment later she was back. 'Dad, it's for you.'

Mr Parker went through and picked up the receiver, while Gail sat down again opposite me.

A few moments passed in silence, and then I said, 'School today?'

'Yeah,' she replied. 'There's always school.'

'It's just I noticed you weren't wearing your uniform.'

'Oh,' she said. 'No. I don't put it on 'til the last moment.'

She glanced at a clock on the shelf, smiled at me and then disappeared into another room. By this time I'd more or less finished breakfast and so I decided to make a move. I was feeling very tired, and despite all the coffee couldn't wait to get back to bed. However, it seemed appropriate to thank Mr Parker for his hospitality, so I got up from my seat and stood waiting by the door. I glanced at the items of mail lying on the shelf, and my eye was caught by a postcard depicting the Taj Mahal. It was very tempting to pick it up and read it, but just then Mr Parker came back into the kitchen.

'Well, that's a good bit of news,' he announced. 'The boats have fetched up at Bryan Webb's place.'

He said 'Bryan Webb' as though I was supposed to know who he was.

'Is that the bloke who goes round in a cardboard crown?' I asked.

'Yes, you'll have seen him in the Packhorse.'

'Plays a lot of darts.'

'Yes, that sounds like Bryan.'

'Well, thanks for the breakfast,' I said. 'Very nice.'

He smiled. 'Do you want to come over to Bryan's and help bring the boats back?'

'How long do you think it'll take?' I asked.

'A couple of hours should see us through.'

After accepting breakfast it would have seemed churlish

not to help, so I agreed. Next thing we were out in the yard heading for Mr Parker's pick-up. We paused to look at the piece of equipment on the trailer. I could now see that it was a circular saw. All the parts were a dull yellow colour, apart from the huge blade, which was quite heavily rusted.

'What do you think of that?' asked Mr Parker.

'Looks useful,' I replied. 'Fits on the back of a tractor, does it?'

'That's right,' he said. 'Picked it up yesterday at the auction.' He rubbed a section of metal and the yellow brightened considerably. 'Should clean up nicely.'

'What about the rust?'

'We'll soon work that off. Now we'll just get the trailer unloaded, then we can get going.'

The circular saw looked far too big for the two of us to lift, but Mr Parker clearly had the matter in hand. He backed the truck over to the trailer, got them hooked together, then went to the big shed and slid open the doors. Next he reversed the whole outfit up the ramp. While he did all this I stood around uselessly, trying not to get in the way. A moment later he beeped his horn, so I walked up the ramp into the shed. The trailer was now neatly positioned under a chain-and-pulley hoist suspended from a roof girder. He'd already got out of the truck and was heaving the circular saw upwards single-handedly, so I rushed over to help. It hardly made any difference as he seemed to be considerably stronger than I was, and next thing the saw was hanging in the air three feet above the trailer.

'Thank you,' said Mr Parker. 'We'll have to get it fixed onto the tractor sometime.'

While he took a moment's rest I cast a quick glance round the inside of the shed. Apart from a substantial-looking tractor nearby, there was a huge array of other equipment as well, including a collection of tyres and wheels, and some welding gear. Quite of lot of spare parts lay here and there too. From where I stood I could see what looked like the front section of a snow plough, the chassis and controls of a caterpillar vehicle, and a concrete mixer with a dismantled engine. Also a large pile of wooden planks. There was more stuff piled up at the back of the shed, and the whole place had a combined smell of lubricating oil, paint and grease. It reminded me more of a factory warehouse than an agricultural building.

'Got some good tackle here,' I remarked.

'Yes,' said Mr Parker. 'It all comes in handy on occasion.'

As the daylight streamed into the shed I saw something gleaming in the far corner. I tried to see what it was, but he was already on the move again.

'Come on,' he said, getting into the pick-up. 'We'd better be getting over to Bryan's.'

I joined him and we set off, leaving the shed doors open. A minute later we arrived at the front gate and turned out onto the road. As we did so I again noticed how bright the green square looked. Mr Parker had fallen silent for the moment, so I decided to start up a conversation to pass the journey.

'Do you ever go to the Packhorse yourself?' I asked.

'Well, I do from time to time,' he said. 'Generally try to avoid it though.'

'Why's that then?'

'Well, I always seem to end up buying everyone else a drink.'

'Oh, right.'

'Costs a fortune some nights.'

'Don't they ever buy you one back then?'

'Yes, I suppose they do,' he said, after giving the question some thought. 'Still costs a fortune though.'

Bryan Webb's place turned out to be one of the properties

we'd passed during our search of the previous night. It was situated on the opposite side of the lake to Mr Parker's, and appeared to be some kind of farm. As we pulled into the front entrance a pervading smell of sheep confirmed this, although there was no sign of any actual animals. Bryan's house was only a few yards from the water's edge. It stood between a number of outbuildings on the one side, and a Dutch barn on the other, in which was parked a flatbed lorry. He emerged from the house when he heard us arrive, wearing his usual cardboard crown. Also a pair of rubber wellington boots.

'Thought it might be you,' he announced, before nodding in my direction. 'I see you've got an assistant.'

'Yes,' replied Mr Parker. 'He's been making himself useful the last couple of days.'

'Smart boy wanted,' said Bryan, giving me a wink. 'Your boats are along here.'

He led us through a gate to the foreshore. There, pulled up on some shingle, lay the seven rowing boats, still attached to their mooring buoy.

'That was a stroke of luck, you noticing them,' said Mr Parker.

'I'll say it was,' replied Bryan. 'I wouldn't normally go to the window at that time in the morning, but Deakin had left the wrong milk again and I was looking across the lake to see how far he'd got.'

'What milk did you ask for then?'

'Well, I prefer homogenized Wednesdays. When my uncle has his tea here.'

'Oh yes, how is Rupert?'

'He's very well, thank you. Been coming over Wednesdays regular and doing a bit of fencing for me. Almost got it all done now.'

'That's good.'

'So, anyway,' Bryan continued, 'I saw Deakin coming down from your place, which meant he'd be going along to Pickthall's next. Thought I'd give them a ring, ask them to intercept him, so to speak. I was just walking through to the phone when strike me pink there were all these boats bumping against my foreshore. I rushed out and got a rope on them and . . . well, there you are.'

Telling this story seemed to take its toll out of Bryan and he sat down on one of the boats for a rest. Meanwhile Mr Parker wandered round giving each of them a brief examination. They were all tied one behind the other with a length of mooring line, and when he got to my boat from the day before he gave the knot I'd tied a little pull, as if checking to see if it held. Then he turned to Bryan.

'Well,' he said. 'We'd better see about getting the trailer through here. Looks like it's going to take three or four journeys to get them all back.'

A few minutes later we had the pick-up and trailer parked on the foreshore, and the three of us began loading the first boat. Only then did I discover that the vessels were designed strictly for floating, not carrying. They seemed to weigh about half a ton each. I knew from my own experience that it was easy sliding one of these boats ashore in shallow water. Lifting it bodily onto a trailer was another matter entirely. There was nothing to hold on to except the gunwales, and we had to get each one up a steep grassy bank from the shingle to where the vehicle was. They were a good fifteen feet long or more, and with room only for two at a time on the trailer, I could see a morning of struggle ahead of us. After a lot of cursing and sweating we managed to get the first one loaded, and then we all stood back to review the situation.

'Wouldn't it be easier just to row them all across?' I suggested.

As soon as I spoke I realized what I'd let myself in for.

Bryan looked at me expectantly, while Mr Parker peered across the lake towards the distant jetty.

'Well, if you're offering, that would be very kind,' he said at length. 'Thank you.'

'Be a nice run-out for you,' commented Bryan. 'Expect you were hoping for another trip in a boat, weren't you?'

'Er . . . yes,' I replied. 'Well, sort of.'

'So you'll do that for us, will you?' asked Mr Parker.

'Course he will,' said Bryan. 'Look at him. He can't wait to get back out on the water.'

'Yeah,' I said. 'That's fine by me.'

And so it was 'arranged' that I would row the six remaining boats across the lake. To tell the truth I didn't really mind because I'd quite enjoyed my excursion the day before, but I soon began wondering how long it would all take. The plan seemed to be that I would row one boat and take the rest in tow behind me. I had a feeling from the start that this wouldn't work, but I went along with it all the same. The two of them helped me cast off and I began pulling the oars, only to find I was getting nowhere quickly. Coming ashore again I got my boots wet for the third time in two days, and we then decided I should try it with fewer boats in tow. After a bit of trial and error I ended up taking three across on the first trip.

'Makes sense really,' said Bryan. 'Three first journey, three second journey.'

While we were messing around getting boats tied together and untied again, with their oars shipped correctly, I began to get the impression that neither Mr Parker nor Bryan Webb had the slightest idea about boating. I ended up doing most of the organization, and when I asked them to grab hold of the gunwales they didn't know what I was talking about. Not that I gained any advantage from my superior knowledge, of course. After all, it was me who had to do the work of actually rowing the string of boats across the lake. Finally I left them behind on the shore and set out on my first journey. The weather was nice again, and although the voyage was very slow it was far from being unpleasant. In fact it turned out to be quite enjoyable, what with the impressive scenery and everything. I hadn't had much sleep overnight, but out here on the water that didn't seem to matter much. When I got halfway I paused for a rest. Then, as I lolled peacefully in the sunshine, I began pondering Bryan's remark about my taking 'another trip in a boat'. I realized he must have seen me out on the lake the previous day, and it struck me that there was very little you could do around here without somebody else knowing about it. As if to confirm this, a movement over at Mr Parker's place caught my eye. I watched as he arrived home with the pick-up and trailer bearing the single boat we'd loaded. He didn't bring it down to the jetty, however, and instead took it up towards the big shed, where I lost sight of him. I continued my break for a few more minutes before pressing on. I'd been half expecting him to come and meet me when I arrived, but after a fruitless wait near the shore I decided to tie the boats on to the jetty and go back for the other three. In doing so I quickly came to the conclusion that Bryan's mathematics were up the creek. It wasn't just a case of moving three boats on each journey, because I had to use one of them to get back over to the other side. Which meant I'd actually be moving four boats on the next trip. With this in mind I paced myself and took it nice and easy on the way back across. There was no sign of Bryan when I got there, so I gathered up the remaining boats and set off again without having a rest. This turned out to be a mistake. Midway across the lake I started to feel thoroughly worn out. My back was beginning to hurt, and my shoulders ached, not to mention the blisters on my hands. This ferrying of boats backwards and forwards might have started off as quite a pleasant task, but it had now turned into a relentless slog. Still, I could hardly abandon the voyage at such a late stage. The end was almost in sight, so I had no choice but to keep on going. When I finally made it to the shore Mr Parker was standing waiting for me.

'That's all of them now, is it?' he asked, as I tied up.

'Yep,' I replied. 'That's the lot.'

'Good.'

'Do you want them left tied to the jetty?'

'No. I think we'll pull them ashore while we're both here.'

'Oh,' I said. 'OK.'

Heaving the six boats ashore used the last of my energy, but it seemed Mr Parker still hadn't finished with me.

'Now then,' he said. 'We've seen what you can do with a paintbrush. What are you like with a hammer and nails?'

'Er . . . well, not too bad,' I replied. ' "Competent" would be the right word, I suppose.'

'So you can hit a nail straight, can you?'

'Most times, yeah.'

' "Cos we've got another little job for you if you're interested.'

'What's that then?'

He indicated the jetty. 'These planks need replacing.'

'Oh yes,' I said. 'I noticed that. They could give way at any moment.'

'So you're in full agreement that the job needs doing?'

'Should be looked at fairly soon, yes.'

'Well, we've got lots of planks up in the shed. They just need cutting down to size, that's all. Have you ever operated a circular saw?'

'No, I haven't. Sorry.'

'That's alright,' he said. 'We can soon give you a run-through. Are you interested then?'

'Yeah, I don't mind having a go at it,' I replied. 'But I could do with a bit of a rest first.'

'Alright. We'll get you started tomorrow, if that's OK.'

'Right.'

'By the way, there's a caravan up in the top yard. You can use it if you wish.'

'Oh, well, no,' I said. 'Thanks anyway, but I'm quite happy in my tent.'

'Plenty of hot water up there as well,' he added.

'Is there?'

'No end of it. You'll be welcome to take as much as you like.'

'Oh . . . er, well, in that case, yes, alright. Thanks.'

'Same arrangement about the rent, of course. Fix the jetty and you can stay there for free.'

This deal didn't seem to balance out properly, but in my exhausted state of mind I couldn't quite think why. Mr Parker then announced that he had to go off somewhere, but that I could move into the caravan immediately.

'Make yourself at home,' he said, before driving away.

After packing my tent, I went up to the top yard. The first thing I noticed when I arrived there was the increased number of oil drums gathered next to the gateway. I'd counted twelve the last time I looked, but now several more had appeared, taking the figure nearer to twenty. Mr Parker was apparently building up his collection.

In a far corner I found the caravan. It was very neat and tidy inside, quite airy, with wooden panelling and old-fashioned gas lamps. I put my bag on the folding bed and flopped down beside it, intending to unpack one or two things. Before doing so I glanced at a pile of journals on the cabinet nearby. They were all copies of a local publication called the *Trader's Gazette*, and I picked one up and began leafing through it.

The newsprint was of cheap quality, but a banner headline claimed a circulation of several thousand. Inside, it was packed with page after page of goods to buy and sell. As well as an extensive classified section, there were also notices for auctions, debt clearances and other forthcoming public sales. The centrefold carried an array of advertisements for garden sheds and greenhouses, with blurred photographs showing what they looked like when assembled. Somewhere near the back I came across special mail-order bargains for extra-durable leather footwear, the price of each illustrated item displayed inside a star, above the encompassing words 'ALL SIZES: M & F.'

For some reason I began working my way through the classifieds to see if there were any boats for sale, and what sort of prices they were likely to change hands for. I ran my eyes down the first column, then the second . . .

*   *   *

When I woke up it was dark, and there was a knocking sound coming from close by. For a moment I couldn't think where I was. A journal lay in my hand and my left leg had developed pins and needles. The knocking came again. When I remembered I was in a caravan I felt my way to the door and opened it. Standing in the darkness was Gail Parker.

'Do you know what the answer to this is?' she asked, shining a torch in my face.

I could see a school exercise book in her hand, and she was holding it open at a certain page.

'Can't see it,' I said. 'Do these lights work?'

'Should do,' she replied. 'Let me have a look.'

I stepped out of the way and she came into the caravan

and felt around for something. Then I heard a gas tap being opened. She struck a match and the lamp above the wash basin lit up. I could now see that she was out of school uniform again. When she'd lit the other lamp she turned and gave me the exercise book.

'Question four,' she said.

I read the question. It was written out in a feminine hand:

4). The ratio of the circumference of a circle to its diameter is known as what?

I glanced at the other questions on the page, some of which had already been attempted. Then I looked up and saw that Gail was watching me intently.

'Do you know what the answer is then?' she asked.

'Yes,' I said. 'Pi.'

'Pie?'

'No. Pi. It's Greek, I think.'

'How's it spelt?'

'Just p . . . i.'

'OK.' She sat down on the folding bed to write in the answer. 'Thanks.'

'That your homework, is it?' I enquired.

'Yes,' she replied. 'Geometry. My dad said you were the best person to ask.'

'Oh,' I said. 'So he knows you're here, does he?'

She nodded vaguely. 'Yeah . . . Is this right?' She was pointing to the next question.

'Well, you've almost got it, but you've spelt hypotenuse wrong.'

I sat down beside her and took her pencil, writing the word correctly inside the book cover.

'Thanks,' she said. 'What about the other questions?'

'Tell you what,' I said. 'Why don't you leave it with me

and I'll have a look through them all. When's it got to be in?'

'Day after tomorrow.'

'Alright, I'll give it you tomorrow night then.'

'OK,' she smiled. 'Thanks.'

She stood up and made ready to depart.

'Aren't you a bit . . . er . . . grown up to be still at school?' I asked.

'I'm younger than I look,' she replied. 'I can leave when I'm sixteen.'

'When's that then?'

'Easter,' she said. 'Anyway, thanks again. Bye.'

'Yeah, bye.'

And a moment later she was gone. I had meant to ask her what time it was, but for some reason I didn't get round to it. Eventually I found my watch buried in the bottom of my bag and discovered that it was nine o'clock. Which meant the pub was only open for two more hours! I ran some water into the basin for a quick wash, and it came out brown for half a minute before turning clear. It remained cold though, and I realized that the hot supply I'd been promised wasn't going to be on tap. I should have known really. After all, this was only a caravan at the end of a farmyard, probably with a hose running to it from one of the outbuildings. If I wanted hot water I was going to have to go over to the house for it. I decided to find out about that in the morning, and make do tonight with a cold wash.

A short while later I was ready to go out. The unscheduled sleep had left me refreshed despite my earlier exertions, so I again set off walking to the pub. As I did so it struck me that I hadn't been anywhere on my motorbike for several days now, apart from moving it up to the top yard during the afternoon. The engine could really have done with having a proper run somewhere. Still, I'd be making up for the lack of use when I hit the road in a day or two. I could hardly see the repairs to the jetty taking any longer than that.

All the talk in the Packhorse that night was about Bryan Webb's discovery of the missing boats. I heard the story repeated several times during the evening as new people came into the bottom bar and demanded to hear all the details. Over and over again he recounted the events leading up to the first sighting: how he wouldn't normally be looking out at that time except that Deakin had left the wrong milk again. I noticed that later versions of the story had Bryan wading out to retrieve the boats, rather than just 'getting a rope on to them' as he'd described earlier. Still, this was his privilege. The episode had turned him into a minor celebrity for the time being, and he was entitled to embellish the facts if he so wished. After much speculation about how the boats had got away in the first place, general agreement was reached that the mooring chain must have broken. No one could remember when it had last been replaced, if ever.

'There's been a mooring there for years,' remarked Bryan. 'But I've no idea when it was first put down.'

'Well, it's lost now,' said another drinker. 'There'll have to be a new one made.'

A secondary discussion then ensued concerning Deakin, and how he sometimes got the orders wrong. The bar stool at the end of the counter had its usual occupant, and he gave his opinion on the matter.

'Well, if you ask me,' he said, 'Deakin's taken on too much work. He's bound to make a mistake occasionally.'

'That's fair enough,' replied Bryan. 'But why's it always *my* milk he gets wrong?'

This caused a certain amount of laughter around the bar.

'Did you ring Pickthall's to intercept him?' someone asked.

'I did after I'd got the boats ashore,' said Bryan, 'but they told me he'd already been and gone.'

'So what did you do then?'

'I rang the dairy and left him a message. He's got until midnight to deliver my homogenized or I'm cancelling all future orders.'

There was more laughter, and Bryan strode triumphantly towards the dartboard. Then, as sets of darts were produced for the evening's play, another buzz went round the pub.

It seemed that Tommy Parker had arrived in the top bar.

4

The first I knew of it was when Tony leaned over the counter and said, 'There's a pint of Ex in the pump for you when you're ready.'

'Where's that come from then?' I asked.

He raised his eyebrows and inclined his head slightly, causing me to glance past him. Beyond the counter in the top bar I saw Mr Parker conversing with the landlord and one or two locals. When he saw me looking he gave me a nod and a quiet smile.

'Courtesy of your boss,' said Tony.

'Er . . . he's not really my boss,' I said. 'I've just been doing some odd jobs for him, that's all.'

Tony smiled. 'Whatever you say.'

I wasn't the only recipient of Mr Parker's generosity. There was apparently also a pint in the pump for Bryan Webb. The man on the bar stool received one as well, even though he'd played no part in the rowing boats' recovery. In the last couple of days I'd gathered that his name was Kenneth, and that he was some kind of mechanic. I guessed this from the number of conversations he had about car engines. He was constantly being asked questions on the subject of carburettors, spark plugs and anti-freeze, to which he always replied, 'Bring it round sometime and I'll have a look at it.'

Shortly after receiving his new pint Kenneth carted it off

to the top bar, announcing that he needed to 'see Tommy about something'.

As the evening continued I glanced from time to time through to where Mr Parker was holding court, and was struck by how important his presence seemed to be. People were continually going up to talk to him, then coming back with looks on their faces that suggested they'd been granted their deepest wish. After half an hour or so it seemed appropriate to buy him a drink in return for the one he'd bought me, so I asked Tony to find out what he'd like.

'He'll have a light ale with you if that's alright,' came the reply.

This seemed very reasonable and I happily forked out the price of the drink. I was surprised, however, when Tony returned with a message from Mr Parker.

'He says have you got that pound you owe him?'

'Er . . . oh, yes,' I said. 'I'd forgotten all about that.'

I handed the money over and Tony took it up to the top bar. This incident could have been embarrassing, but most people's attention was now on the darts, and nobody took any notice. I decided to put it out of mind, and went and chalked my name up on the blackboard.

A little later Tony let it be known that the final drops of Topham's Excelsior Bitter had at last been consumed, and that there were only keg and bottled beers left. I looked at my empty glass and reflected that it was a good job I was leaving in a couple of days' time.

Walking back to the campsite after the pub closed I heard again the distant chime from across the lake. Yes, it was definitely 'Half a pound of treacle'. A moment later I caught a glimpse of the faraway vehicle with its faintly glowing lights. It was moving along the road somewhere near Bryan Webb's place.

*   *   *

Next morning I found Mr Parker in the big shed amidst a
flurry of blue sparks. These were accompanied by a sharp
crackling noise. I watched for a while, shielding my eyes until
the sparks subsided. Then I saw that he was busy welding
some winch-gear onto the front of his trailer. It looked like
he'd been having a bit of a sort out inside the shed. The boat
we'd moved the day before was now resting on some wooden
blocks nearby, and there was quite a lot of space cleared
around it. When he saw me standing there he lowered his
welding mask.

'Morning,' he said. 'Just thought I'd get this done while I
had the time.'

'Looks like it could be useful,' I remarked.

'Yes, a winch can be very handy. I'll be finished in a
minute. Pass me a new rod, will you, please?'

I stood watching as he completed the work, and then he
moved the welding equipment out of the way.

'Right, we'll give it a quick test.'

There was a length of cable wrapped around the winch
drum, with a hook attached to one end. Mr Parker gave me
the hook and got me to pull it away across the shed to a
distance of about thirty feet. Then he cranked a handle and
wound me back in again, until the hook settled against the
winch housing.

'That seems to work alright,' he said. 'Now then, are you
ready to learn about this saw?'

'Ready as ever,' I replied.

'Good. I'll move the tractor and we can get it fixed on.'

The circular saw remained suspended on the hoist where

we'd left it. Mr Parker climbed onto the tractor, started up and manoeuvred it into position. I could see that there were some fixing points on the saw which presumably corresponded with others on the back of the tractor, but unfortunately I didn't know what went where. As a result Mr Parker had to do most of the connecting up himself, which meant him getting on and off the tractor several times. During the process there were occasional moments when I thought impatience was going to get the better of him. His voice became raised with frustration as he gave his orders, and this seemed to indicate an oncoming crisis. The trouble was, I'd never operated such machinery before and had little idea how it worked. Mr Parker, on the other hand, was obviously well versed in such matters, and couldn't see why I found any of it difficult. Even when he asked me to lower the hoist slightly I managed to pull it the wrong way so it went upwards instead of down, nettling him yet more.

After ten minutes, however, we had the saw properly connected to the tractor, and he was at ease again. Then he went round the apparatus with a grease gun, applying lubricant to all the bearings. Finally he turned to me.

'Now, I don't need to tell you that this is a piece of highly dangerous equipment,' he said. 'So I think we'd better start with a short demonstration.'

He waved me out of the way and then reached over to the tractor. I heard a clunk as he engaged the driving gear, and instantly the huge blade began to turn. After regulating the engine speed he took a plank from the nearby pile. Carefully positioning his feet, he ran the plank across the blade, cutting it into two. After repeating this a couple of times he stood back and let me have a go at it. Then he showed me how to cut a plank properly to size by making certain adjustments. All the time he kept reminding me to keep well away from the blade because, as he himself pointed out, the safety cover was missing.

'It must have gone astray sometime in the past,' was his only explanation.

He disengaged the power and the blade spun slowly to a halt. Then the two of us set about loading planks onto the trailer, until there were enough to replace all the old ones on the jetty.

'Driven a tractor before?' he asked.

No, I replied, I hadn't. There next followed a short lesson in how to drive a tractor. Finally we were ready to go. I drove slowly down to the lake, and Mr Parker followed in his pick-up with the trailer in tow. When we arrived beside the jetty he produced a selection of tools from his cab. These included a hammer, a small crowbar and a handsaw. There was also a box of nails.

'Right,' he said. 'I'll just get you started and then the job's all yours.'

He seized the crowbar and jammed it under the first plank on the jetty, giving it a deft twist. There was a creaking noise and the plank lifted a little. He then repeated the action at the other end. A moment later the plank had come away and he threw it to one side before starting on the next one.

When he'd removed another three or four he turned to me and said, 'Well, that's easy enough done. I think I can leave you to it now. Be careful with that saw bench, won't you?'

'I'll try to be,' I replied with a grin. 'Otherwise it'll only be me who regrets it.'

He smiled vaguely and gave me a nod before climbing into his truck and driving away. Then I took the crowbar and set about removing the next plank. I discovered straight away that the task wasn't as simple as Mr Parker had made it look. Several attempts were required just to get the crowbar in the right position, and even then the plank refused to yield without a fight. When it did finally come away it was in several broken pieces. I realized again that Mr Parker was much stronger than me, despite being perhaps twenty years older. He'd most likely been doing manual work around the place all his life, and it showed. Tools and equipment seemed to be obedient in his hands, whereas I always had a struggle of some kind or other. Still, I had a feeling that the job would become more straightforward as I got used to it, so I pressed on. An hour later I'd successfully removed about a dozen planks. Whoever fixed them on in the first place had certainly done a good job and many of the nails were proving to be particularly steadfast, even though they were quite rusty. Nevertheless, I was beginning to get the better of them. I decided it was now time to cut some new timber. I started up the tractor, walked round it a couple of times to make sure everything looked right, and then engaged the drive. As the saw blade began turning I took a plank from the pile and marked the correct length and width, using one of the old planks as a template. Then I began sawing. To my surprise the first piece of cut timber came out exactly the right size. I was so pleased with it that I stopped the saw and went straight to the jetty to get it nailed on. Suddenly I had a picture of what the completed job would look like. I was rebuilding a jetty at the edge of a lake, and realized that in this way I would be leaving my mark on the place. If I ever returned I could come to the waterside and examine my handiwork to see how it was lasting against the elements. Maybe point the jetty out to someone and say, 'It was me who built that.'

Or rebuilt it anyway.

I spent the rest of the morning cutting planks and fixing them in position, before prising off some more of the old ones. It had slowly dawned on me as the hours passed that this wasn't going to be a quick job that I could knock off in one day, but that didn't seem important any more as I was quite enjoying it. I had no idea how much Mr Parker was planning to pay me for this work as we hadn't discussed the matter, but presumably he had a figure in mind based on how long it took to complete. No doubt I'd find out what it was in due course. Meanwhile, I was feeling slightly peckish, so I walked up to the caravan and had something to eat. There was no sign of Mr Parker or his pick-up truck, so I guessed he was out on some business or other. His absence made the yard seem very quiet. For one moment I was tempted to go and poke around in the big shed to see what else was stored there, but I thought I had better not in case he suddenly came back. Instead I strolled down to the lake and continued work.

It was an hour later while I was busy cutting some more timber that I realized I had a visitor. I'd just turned round to select a new plank from the pile when I became aware of an elderly man standing at the edge of the trees, watching. He gave no sign of acknowledgement, however, so I carried on with what I was doing. The combined din of the tractor and the circular saw tended to isolate me from the rest of the world, and I was also keeping a constant eye on the spinning blade. As a result I had no idea how long he'd been there. Presumably he'd come across me by chance while out for a lakeside walk. I expected him to move on at any moment, but when I again glanced towards the trees I saw that he'd come a little closer. After a while he was near enough for me to give him a friendly nod. He responded by offering the next plank and holding it steady as I measured it. Then, while I was getting it cut, he took the template and marked another plank in advance. Then another one after that. This saved me quite a bit of time, and a few minutes later I had several more pieces of timber ready. I shut the saw down and switched the tractor off, turning to the old man as the noise faded.

'Thanks,' I said. 'That was a great help.'

'About time this job was done,' he replied.

'Yes,' I agreed. 'It wouldn't have been safe to leave it much longer.'

'That other lad should have done it while he was here.'

'What other lad?'

'The one who was helping with the boats.'

'Oh,' I said. 'You mean Bryan Webb.'

'That fool who goes round in the cardboard crown?'

'Er . . . yeah.'

'No,' said the old man. 'I'm not talking about him.'

'Well,' I replied. 'I don't really know anyone else.'

He shook his head with impatience. 'There was a lad here during the summer, supposed to be looking after the boats. Idle perisher, he was.'

'Was he?'

'Never did a stroke.'

'Oh,' I said. 'I didn't know they had someone doing that.'

'As soon as there was any proper work to be done he took off. Last thing he did was paint that hut, and you can see what a pig's ear he made of it.'

I glanced towards the hut and remembered the problems we'd had getting the hatch open a couple of days ago.

'Yes,' I remarked. 'I noticed the paintwork was a bit slapdash.'

'Bit slapdash?' snapped the old man. 'He shouldn't have been allowed anywhere near a paintbrush!'

'No, suppose not.'

'You look like you'd do a much better job.'

'Thanks.'

'Shame you had to go and spill green all over Parker's gateway though.'

'Oh . . . er . . . yes.'

'Still, at least you had the sense to make it into a square.' He now turned his attention to the pile of planks. 'Good load of timber, this.'

'I don't really know anything about it.'

'Well, take my word for it,' he said. 'It's good.'

Shortly afterwards I resumed work on the jetty. The elderly man seemed to know something about joinery and stayed to help out for a while, positioning the planks and occasionally adding a few extra nails here and there. As the afternoon progressed, however, he began to show signs of tiredness, and eventually wandered off after telling me I was doing a 'reasonable' job. I thanked him for his help and said goodbye before he receded into the trees. Then I got back to work.

The light was beginning to fade when Mr Parker appeared in his pick-up truck. He got out and walked onto the jetty, pressing the new planks with his boots and generally carrying out a thorough examination. Meanwhile, I watched and awaited his verdict.

'I thought you'd have got a bit further than this,' he said at length.

'Should get it finished tomorrow,' I replied.

'That's alright then. Can you put the tractor in the shed overnight, please?'

'OK.'

He went over to the pick-up and got the grease gun, before going round the machinery once again to treat all the moving parts. When he'd finished I started up the tractor and set off towards the shed. By the time I got back to the caravan darkness was falling and I felt like I'd done a good day's work. I had a cup of tea and then went over to the house to see about getting some hot water, taking Gail Parker's completed homework with me. It was she who answered the door.

'Here you are,' I said. 'Shouldn't be any mistakes now.'

'Thanks,' she said with a smile, putting the exercise book to one side without even glancing at it.

'Is there any chance of a bucket of hot water, so I can get a wash?'

'You can get it from the boiler room,' she replied. 'Just a sec.'

She took a key from a hook and led me round the foot of the house to another outside door. Unlocking it, she went inside and turned on the light.

'You'll probably find it quite hot in here,' she remarked as I followed her in.

In the dim light I could see a large boiler throbbing away in the middle of the room, beneath a black aluminium flue. There were a number of water pipes leading up to the ceiling, and one of them had a tap plumbed into it.

'Got a bucket?' asked Gail.

'Oh,' I said. 'Er . . . no.'

'There's one there.'

I turned and saw a bucket in the corner and went to reach for it. At the same moment Gail squeezed past me to do the same thing.

'Sorry,' I said as we bumped together.

'That's alright,' she said, smiling as she handed it to me. 'Will you be wanting any more after this?'

'Any more what?'

'Hot water.'

'Might do, yes,' I replied.

'Right, I'll see if I can find you a spare key.'

'Thanks.'

She left me filling the bucket and went out. I thought she'd be coming straight back so I waited a while, but after ten minutes there was no sign of her. I eventually gave up and returned to the caravan, where I enjoyed the luxury of my first wash and shave in hot water for several days. Then I perused the *Trader's Gazette* over supper before going out for the evening.

During the day I'd decided it might be nice to visit Millfold's other pub before leaving the area, just for a change of scenery. I hadn't gone there before because it didn't look as lively as the Packhorse, and seemed to cater for more staid types of people. Nevertheless, I thought it might be worth giving a try. It was called the Ring of Bells and occupied the opposite side of the square, next door to Hodge's shop.

It came as no surprise to find that Hodge was one of the few customers. He showed some sign of recognition when I walked in, and murmured something to the landlord before greeting me with a nod. He was sitting at the end of the counter with a whisky glass. Another man occupied a stool some distance away, and there were two others sitting at a table by the window, but apart from these people the place was deserted. The landlord seemed friendly enough, however, and took a beer glass from the shelf the moment he saw me.

'Pint of?' he asked.

'Got any Topham's Excelsior?'

'I'm afraid not,' he said. 'Not enough demand for it round here.'

'Oh, OK,' I said. 'Pint of lager then, please.'

'Right you are.'

While the landlord was pouring my drink, Hodge decided to start up a conversation.

'On the bike tonight?' he asked.

'No,' I replied. 'Prefer to walk.'

'Don't use it much, do you?'

'Not for short journeys, no.'

'Haven't seen you out and about on it for several days.'

'No, well, I've been busy.'

'But I thought you were supposed to be on holiday.'

'Yes, you're right,' I said. 'I am.'

To tell the truth, I found this Hodge bloke quite irritating and was beginning to regret coming into the Ring of Bells. After all, it wasn't much of a pub as far as atmosphere went. There was no dartboard, no raucous character in a cardboard crown, and no subtle division between top and bottom bar. All there was were these people sitting around sipping whisky and asking banal questions. Alright, so the Packhorse wasn't exactly the centre of the galaxy, but it beat the Ring of Bells hands down for entertainment value. I spent a dull evening wondering what it would be like living here if this was the only pub, and made a mental note not to bother coming back.

* * *

I was down by the lakeside quite early next morning, determined to get the jetty finished the same day. I saw Mr Parker looking out of his kitchen window as I went off on the tractor, but he didn't come out. In fact I didn't see him to speak to until the evening. Meanwhile I pressed on with the repairs. By now I had grown quite adept at removing the old planks, and was also much more confident when operating the circular saw. Sometime in the afternoon the old man turned up again, and he was soon lending a hand. I didn't know whether he'd come back on purpose or just happened to be passing by, but either way he helped speed the work up considerably. At the same time there was no question that I would need to reward him for his efforts. As far as I could make out he was helping because, like me, he had nothing better to do. We finished the job just before dusk, and once again he wandered off without saying goodbye. I then began packing the tools away and gathered up the remaining planks to take them back to the yard. Finally, when it was all done, I went and stood on the end of the jetty and gazed out across the lake.

During the day I'd detected a change in the climate. It appeared that the sunny weather was over for good, and now a slight breeze was starting up. The water had a grey look about it which no longer suggested a pleasant after-noon's boating. The sky too was grey, and the fells seemed to be looming rather closely. It struck me that this was just about the right time to be moving on. After a while I heard a vehicle approaching, and turned round to see Mr Parker's truck pulling onto the shore. Piled in the back were a number of empty oil drums. He approached and joined me on the jetty.

'Did you say you were leaving tomorrow?' he asked.

'Yes,' I replied. 'That's the plan anyway.'

'Well, you'll need to get away early,' he said. 'We've got some rain coming.'

'Yes, I thought it looked a bit gloomy.'

'The weatherman says the isobars are closing in.'

'Does he?'

'It's 978, falling rapidly.'

'Oh,' I said. 'Right.'

Mr Parker had been peering at the opposite shore of the lake, but now he turned to me.

'You'll not have seen it rain here, will you?'

'It did rain a bit the other day, yes.'

'That was nothing,' he said. 'You haven't seen this place until you've seen it rain properly.'

'No, I suppose not.'

'Teems down, it does.'

'I bet.'

'So I'd get away early if I were you.'

'OK.'

And with that he turned and made his way back to the truck. We loaded the spare planks between the oil drums, then he drove off while I followed in the tractor.

I was slightly disconcerted that he'd made no mention of how much he was going to pay me, but it occurred to me that there was no particular hurry as I wasn't leaving until the next day.

More disappointing was the fact that he hadn't remarked on the quality of my workmanship. It didn't bother me unduly, but it would have been nice if he'd at least said something about it. Even if it was just to note that I'd sawn all the timber straight.

Then I realized that it was probably no big deal to him, nothing more than another job finished and out of the way. The last thing he was going to do was heap praise on someone for doing a bit of joinery.

After we'd put the gear in the shed, however, he paused by the door.

'I've been thinking,' he said. 'I probably owe you something for that work you've done for me.'

'Er . . . well, it doesn't matter really,' I replied.

'Of course it does,' he declared. 'It was quite remiss of us not making a proper arrangement beforehand.'

'Suppose it was.'

'So I really must let you have something before you leave.'

'Right.'

He indicated the green petrol pump beside the shed.

'How would you like me to fill your tank up?'

'Oh . . . OK,' I said. 'If that's alright with you.'

'Of course it is,' he said. 'That's the least I can offer.'

I went round and got my bike, and he squeezed two and half gallons into the petrol tank.

'Thanks,' I said.

'Don't mention it,' he replied. 'I hope you've been comfortable in the caravan, have you?'

'Oh,' I said quickly. 'Yes, it was very kind of you.'

'That's good.'

He locked the pump and then turned to me.

'Right. Well, I might not see you when you leave, so have a good trip and come back sometime if you can.'

We shook hands and he headed across to his house, where I noticed the lights inside had already been turned on for the evening. This gave it a very warm, comfortable appearance and made the rest of the yard seem fairly bleak in comparison. When I got round to my caravan I realized the wind was increasing steadily. Somewhere in the mounting gloom I could hear an irregular clanging that suggested one of the corrugated sheets on the big shed had come loose. Several times during the next hour I went out to see if I could identify the exact source of the noise, but it was soon too dark to see. I decided there was probably nothing much wrong anyway. No doubt Mr Parker knew about the problem and would get it fixed in his own good time. Meanwhile, I set about preparing some supper. After that I planned to get my stuff packed and work out what I'd need for the journey next day. One particular item was of great importance. Somewhere in the bottom of my bag lay a set of waterproofs, and I was thankful I'd remembered to bring them.

With the wet weather gathering outside it was odd to think that when I first arrived here it had still felt like summer. That seemed a long time ago now, but actually it was less than a fortnight. I was trying to imagine what an entire winter would be like when a knock came on the caravan door. It was Gail.

'I've brought you the spare key to the boiler room,' she said.

'Oh thanks,' I replied. 'Er ... you know I'm going tomorrow, do you?'

'Yeah, but I thought you might like some hot water tonight.'

'Oh right. Well, thanks again.'

She remained standing in the doorway.

'Is there anything else?' I asked.

'Yes,' she said. 'They've set this essay at school and I don't know how to do it.'

Just then the wind caught the door and slammed it back against the caravan.

'Come in a sec,' I said. 'It's getting cold out there.'

She stepped inside and I reached round and closed the door.

'Now what's this essay about?'

'It's called "Where I live".'

'Is that the title?'

'Yeah.'

'So it's got to be a description really.'

'Yeah.'

'Well,' I said. 'I'd have thought that would be fairly straightforward.'

'Why?'

'"Cos you live somewhere quite interesting, don't you? With the fells and the sheep and everything. And the lake.'

'What's so interesting about that?'

'Well, nothing really, I suppose. But it should be easy enough to describe.'

'So what do I put then?'

While we were speaking I'd become aware that she had a rough exercise book in her hand. She now opened it and stood ready with a pencil.

'You want some suggestions, do you?'

'Please,' she said.

'OK, you could start with, "*I live in a place . . .*" No, hang on. "*The place where I live is . . .*" Er . . . maybe it would be better if you were sitting down.'

'Alright then.'

'Tell you what, you sit there and I'll stand here.'

'OK.'

She sat down on the folding bed, while I moved to the opposite side of the caravan before resuming.

'Right, ready?'

'Yeah.'

'"*The place where I live is different to many other places.*" '

I paused while she wrote it down.

'No, wait a sec. Change that to "*different from many other places.*" '

She tutted. 'Couldn't you just write it and I'll copy it out after?'

'What, you mean you want me to do the whole thing?'

'Yeah,' she said. 'You'll be better at it than me.'

'Well, I was planning to go out tonight.'

She smiled. 'It won't take you long.'

'No, I suppose not,' I said. 'But you might have trouble with my handwriting.'

'I expect I'll be alright.'

I thought about it for a moment. 'OK then, I'll do a basic version and you'll have to tidy it up.'

'Thanks.'

'I'll leave it on the shelf here.'

'Right.' She rose from the bed and went to the doorway before giving me another smile. 'Thanks again.'

'Er . . . when did you say you were sixteen?' I asked.

'Easter,' she replied.

'Oh well, happy birthday in advance.'

'Thanks, bye.'

And she disappeared into the night.

I spent about three-quarters of an hour writing that essay, but I probably could have done it in ten minutes if I'd had to. It was a piece of cake really, as easy as painting by numbers. I simply described the maroon boats at rest near the wooded margins of the lake, and the looming fells brooding in the autumn gloom. There was also a bit at the end about the fulsome moon waxing against a starry backdrop, which I thought sounded quite nice. Then I fetched a bucket of hot water, had a wash and went out. I didn't want to drink too much tonight, so I decided to take the motorbike for a change. When I got to Millfold I parked it in the square and entered the Packhorse through the front door. As I passed by the top bar I noticed it was fairly quiet, but this deficit was made up for in the bottom one, which seemed to be quite full, although I didn't recognize many faces. The moment I walked in I was greeted by Gordon from behind the counter.

'Glad you've turned up,' he said. 'We're playing the Journeyman at darts tonight, and we're a man short. Can you help us out?'

'Well,' I replied. 'I'm not very experienced at match play.'

'That's alright. We just want you to make the numbers up.'

I glanced round the crowded bar. 'Doesn't anyone else want to play?'

'They're all from the Journeyman,' said Gordon.

'Well, I'm not a local,' I said.

'Don't worry about that. You've been in here enough times to qualify.'

'Oh, OK then. Where is the Journeyman anyway?'

'Wainskill, about ten miles up the road.'

In this unexpected way I was roped in for a full-scale Inter-Pub League darts match. It came as no surprise to find that

Bryan Webb was captain of the Packhorse team. Tony was supposed to be vice-captain, but because his father had been called away somewhere his services were required behind the counter to assist Gordon. Which was why they needed my help. Bryan quickly adopted me into his side and introduced me to the rest of the team, which included the mechanic Kenneth. As it happened, they all seemed to know who I was anyway, and spoke to me as if we'd been acquainted for years.

It was a good night. The players and their supporters from the Journeyman were numerous enough to give the match a proper competitive atmosphere, and to my surprise I won two of my games. I also noticed that there were quite a few women present, including the one I'd seen talking to Gordon and Tony on previous occasions. After a while I gathered that she was a sort of player-manager for the Journeyman team, and that she'd been over the other night to go through the arrangements for the match. It didn't take long to find out her name was Lesley.

'Shame we haven't got any Ex for you,' remarked Gordon when I went to the bar for my second pint of keg beer.

'Good job really,' I said. 'Otherwise I might have ended up staying here for ever.'

'Oh yes,' he said. 'That's right, you're leaving tomorrow, aren't you?'

'That's the plan.'

'Well I should try to get away as early as possible. We've got some rain coming.'

The increasingly murky climate outside the Packhorse was easily forgotten on an evening like this. Everyone was getting stuck into the drink as usual, and I began to regret bringing my bike since it meant I couldn't have any more after this. As the darts match progressed I also started to realize that Lesley was paying me quite a bit of attention.

Whatever part of the bar I was in, I noticed that she would soon be standing nearby. Once or twice I tried moving around to see what happened, and each time she moved too, although not obviously enough for anyone else to detect. When victory fell at last to the home side and all the players were going round shaking hands with one another, she came up to me.

'Nice game,' she said. 'Can I buy you a drink?'

'Er . . . no thanks,' I replied. 'Any more and I'll be over the limit. Thanks anyway.'

She smiled. 'Maybe another time.'

'Probably not,' I said. 'I'm leaving tomorrow.'

'Going anywhere interesting?'

'Yeah, India.'

'Really?' Her eyes sparkled.

'Yeah, I'm thinking of going overland. You know, Turkey and Persia, that way.'

'Sounds fantastic.'

'Have you done much travelling yourself?'

'Not yet,' she said. 'Just waiting for the chance.'

'Oh, right.'

'You sure you don't want that drink?'

'Yeah, sure . . . thanks.'

Quietly I cursed my luck. What a wasted opportunity! This would have to happen on my last night in the place, and on the only occasion I'd come out on the bike. Next thing Lesley had rejoined her team-mates and our brief conversation was over. I slipped out of the pub shortly afterwards without bothering to say goodbye to anyone. There were now heavy drops of rain on the wind, which was becoming progressively more blustery. When I got back to Hillhouse I remembered Mr Parker's offer about putting my bike in one of the sheds. I should really have taken him up on it when I had the chance, but it was too late now. The whole place was in darkness when I pulled into the top yard, and I guessed that all the doors would be locked for the night. I parked by the caravan and went inside. Lighting the gas lamp I happened to glance at the shelf where I'd left Gail's essay. It was gone.

5

I didn't sleep well that night. For some reason the beer made me sweat a lot, and I kept waking up all in a tangle. The wind was no help either. It continued to work on the loose sheet of corrugated steel, causing it to clang spasmodically for hour after hour. In fact the whole shed now seemed to be creaking in sympathy with the increasing gusts. It must have been well into the early hours before I drifted off properly, and next thing I knew there was daylight coming through the caravan window. More noticeable, though, was the rain drumming on the roof. It was very tempting to turn over and go back to sleep, but I knew I had to get going before the weather worsened even more. Somehow I dragged myself out of bed. I'd used up the last of my food supplies the previous evening, and planned to get a few miles behind me before stopping somewhere for breakfast. I unrolled my waterproofs. They were dry and stiff, and I realized it was a long time since I'd last had cause to use them.

When everything was ready I went outside and started the bike. It had been out in the rain all night, but fortunately seemed to be running OK. Then, after a quick check round the caravan, I set off. There was no sign of activity in the bottom yard or the house as I passed by, nor did I see anyone on the road to Millfold. The rain was coming down hard now, and it struck me as a daft day to be travelling. All the same I had no inclination to alter my plans. I'd had enough of the place, nice as it was, and now wanted to get moving. It was just tough luck that it happened to be raining the day I'd chosen to leave. Besides, I had a feeling that I only had to go fifty or sixty miles and I'd probably run into better weather. A few minutes later I passed the Packhorse and the Ring of Bells, both with their shutters firmly closed, before crossing the bridge and joining the road southward. For a moment I caught a glimpse of Mr Parker's house on the opposite side of the lake, and then it was lost from sight. The only place I knew beyond that was Bryan Webb's. Again there was nobody to be seen as I went by. Not long afterwards the rainwater began running down my neck. Motorcycling was a wretched affair in these conditions, and I prepared myself for a long and dismal journey. I'd read somewhere that the lake was supposed to be nine miles in length, but I knew from my previous trips that the road distance was much further. There were no end of twists and turns, and I'd clocked up more than twenty miles before I finally left the lake behind. This had taken almost an hour, because of having to slow right down on the bends. Now I began climbing as I headed for the first mountain pass. As I did so I wondered why I hadn't simply gone north from Millfold and then picked up the motorway. That would have been much easier than slogging along this twisty road. On the other hand, if I had taken the motorway I'd have had to contend with the spray from all those juggernauts. In truth, whatever way I went I was going to get soaked, and at least the route I'd chosen was traffic-free today.

Unfortunately, there were a lot of puddles, and as I came down the other side of the pass I hit one right in the middle. At that moment I realized my waterproofs were pretty ineffective. But worse than that, the engine stopped. It coughed and spluttered several times before cutting out completely. I rolled to a halt, then gave the starter a kick.

Nothing.

I tried again, with hopes sinking. I already had a suspicion about what the problem might be. It was confirmed when I removed the points cover from the engine and rainwater came running out. This meant I was going to have to sit for hours waiting for the points to dry off.

That's handy, I thought.

There was no shelter here, no trees or buildings, only grassy slopes rising up into the wet mist. Vainly I tried kicking the bike over again, but without success. The thought then came into my mind that I could push it along until I got to somewhere less exposed. Maybe I'd even find a nice dry café just along the road where I could sit and wait. I quickly dismissed this idea, though, as I knew for a fact that there wasn't anything for miles, apart from scattered farms and the occasional private residence. So I stayed where I was, and paced around idly watching rivulets form at the edge of the road. From time to time a vehicle would go by, the driver glancing momentarily in my direction before passing on. Then, after about twenty minutes, a school minibus approached. It was similar to the one I'd seen Gail boarding each morning at the front gate, but I noticed immediately that the occupants were wearing a different-coloured uniform. As the minibus slowed down for the next bend I was aware of a dozen pink faces looking out at me.

There then followed a prolonged spell during which I began to wonder what exactly I was going to do. The rain showed no sign of easing up, and the bike still refused to start. Yet there was no point in abandoning it and going to look for help. After all, nothing actually needed repairing. It just required a chance to dry out. Again I thought how foolish it was to be travelling by motorcycle on a day like this.

After another ten minutes had passed I heard a vehicle approaching from the south. I glanced towards the bend as it appeared, and instantly recognized Mr Parker's pick-up with the trailer in tow. He pulled up beside me.

'You seem to be getting quite attached to the area,' he remarked, by way of greeting.

'Engine's stopped,' I replied.

'I thought you were going to get away early.'

'I did.'

'No,' he said. 'That was nowhere near early enough.'

He got out and looked at the bike.

'The points got wet,' I explained.

He nodded. 'Always the same with these old machines. They let the water in too easily.'

'Just needs to dry out.'

'Well, it'll never get dry here.'

'Doesn't look that way.'

'Not in a month of Sundays.' A moment passed, and then he added, 'Tell you what, why don't we take it home and put it in my shed?'

'Don't you mind?' I asked.

'Of course not,' he said. 'Can't leave you here, can I?'

I couldn't see what choice I had. This was the first time the bike had ever let me down. Now I was stuck and Mr Parker offered the best remedy, so I decided to accept. A few minutes later we had the bike loaded onto his trailer and were on our way north again. The cab heater was turned on full, and very soon there was steam rising from my damp waterproofs.

'Been anywhere interesting?' I asked.

'Had a delivery to make,' he replied. 'Bit of business, you know. Quite fortunate you breaking down where you did.'

'Yeah, suppose so.'

'I always think a journey's more worthwhile if I get a return load as well.'

'Oh . . . er . . . yeah,' I said. 'That's one way of looking at it.'

Sometime later when we passed Bryan Webb's place Mr Parker slowed down and peered towards the property. I couldn't see what he was looking at exactly, but as far as I could make out his attention was focused on the flatbed lorry parked in Bryan's Dutch barn. He didn't pass comment on it, however, and we had soon passed by. After another twenty-five minutes we arrived in his top yard.

'Welcome back,' he said.

'Thanks.'

'If you like you can put your bike in the big shed. That'll be best for getting it dry.'

'Alright.'

'Maybe we should get Kenneth Turner to give it a look-over before you go off anywhere again.'

'I don't think it'll be worth it,' I said. 'I'm sure there's nothing seriously wrong.'

'Well, have a think about it anyway.'

'OK.'

I walked over to the shed and slid the doors back. Immediately I detected the same semi-industrial smell that had hung over the place before, and it gave me an odd sense of returning to somewhere familiar. Glancing within I saw that two rows of wooden blocks had been laid out in the middle of the floor, next to the boat we'd moved the other day. I wheeled the bike inside and left it in a space between the concrete mixer and the dismantled caterpillar vehicle. Something seemed to have gone missing since the last time I was in there, but for the moment I couldn't think what it was. I was still peering round the place when Mr Parker joined me in the doorway.

'Should be enough room for the other boats,' he said.

'Do you keep them all in here during the winter then?' I asked.

'Yes, they need to be under cover really.'

'Yeah, spose.'

'Perhaps you'd like to help me get them moved up here?'

'Sure,' I replied. 'It's the least I can do after all your help.'

'Well, shall we start right away?'

'Yeah, that's fine by me.'

As we returned to the truck I noticed for the first time that the rain had stopped, and that the sky looked far less foreboding than it had earlier. By the time we'd driven down to the lake it even seemed possible that the sun might come out. The six boats were lying where we'd left them. Mr Parker reversed his trailer into position and we hauled two of them on board, using the new winch attachment. When we got back to the shed they had to be transferred onto the wooden blocks. I thought this was going to be a bit of a heave, but he simply jacked the trailer up and shoved the boats roughly off the back. I winced as they slid onto the concrete, but their construction was so solid that they weren't even marked. Then it was just a matter of lifting them a little and shuffling the blocks underneath. He seemed to have the whole process worked out beforehand, and this made it very simple. All the same, I was beginning to feel a bit worn out after we'd completed three such journeys, and I think I must have grunted under the strain as we shifted the final boat.

This caused Mr Parker to remark, 'You're not very strong, are you?'

'Well, I'm not weak either,' I protested. 'I've done quite a lot of heavy lifting actually.'

'When was that?' he asked.

'I used to work on the loading bay at the factory.'

'I thought you said you were in the paint shop.'

'I was eventually. But I started off on the loading bay.'

'So you've done painting and loading,' he said. 'What else?'

'Well, nothing really. Apart from a bit of joinery.'

'Are you a trained joiner then?'

'Er . . . no.'

'What about plumbing? Do you know anything about that?'

'No, 'fraid not.'

'I can do plumbing,' he announced. 'And welding. In fact, there's very little I can't do when I think about it. I know about land drainage, tree planting, fencing and timber felling. I can change the hydraulic pipes on most types of tractor, and I do all my own vehicle maintenance too. That's petrol *and* diesel, mind. In the past I've done ploughing, milking and sheep drenching, as well as dipping. I've installed septic tanks. I know the inner workings of the Watford Slurry Pump. I built this shed we're standing in, and I put down most of the concrete you can see around the place.'

While he was telling me all this I stood beside the boats nodding vaguely. I wasn't sure what it was supposed to be leading up to, but it seemed interesting enough in its own way.

'I can operate circular saws, mechanical excavators, jack-hammers and pile-drivers,' he added, before pausing to give me a significant look. 'But the one subject I know nothing about is boats.'

'Oh,' I said. 'Don't you?'

'Nothing at all.'

'Well I only know a bit myself.'

'Maybe so, but I can see you appreciate them more than I do.'

'I do quite like them, yes.'

He placed his hands in his pockets and stared at the floor.

'The thing is,' he said. 'I want them painting, and I'd like you to do it.'

'But that's a big project,' I replied. 'They'll need several coats to do them properly.'

'That's alright. We've got plenty of paint.'

'And it might turn out they need some caulker too.'

He looked up. 'Caulker?'

'To prevent them leaking.'

'There you are,' he said. 'I wouldn't have known that. I've never even heard of caulker. You're just the man for the job.'

While we talked a thin shaft of sunlight had begun to play on one of the boats. It seemed that the wet weather outside was indeed giving way to clearer, brighter conditions. In this acute light the gold paint along the boat's gunwale momentarily regained a little of its original lustre, giving it a very striking appearance. There was no doubt that the paintwork was in some need of refurbishment, but for a few seconds I had a picture of what the finished job would look like. I could just imagine the raised prow when its details had been carefully touched in by hand, and the gold lines running from stem to stern. Yes, I thought, the completed vessel would look magnificent.

'Trouble is,' I said, 'it'd take weeks to do all seven of them.'

'But you could have them done by Christmas, could you?' asked Mr Parker.

'Well, probably, yes. But I really should get going very soon.'

He ignored my weak protest. 'We've got a bothy you could stay in, if you wished.'

'Oh,' I said. 'Er . . . have you?'

'Across the yard there. Quite cosy in the winter, it is. And we'd give you breakfast every day.'

'Sounds nice.'

'Cooked by Gail, of course.'

I considered his proposition and realized my resistance was

running quite low. To tell the truth I felt exhausted. The waterproofs I'd been wearing for hours were now dry again, but the thought of repeating this morning's journey was unappealing. On the other hand the offer of a place to stay with a cooked breakfast each morning seemed very attractive.

'Can I keep the bike in here for the time being?' I asked.

'Of course you can,' he replied.

'Alright,' I said. 'I'll stay.'

*   *   *

A few minutes later he took me across the yard to see the bothy. It was a tiny place, with a tiny bathroom. As we walked in it felt a bit chilly, but as Mr Parker demonstrated with the flick of an electric switch, it could warm up quite quickly. From one of the windows there was a good view of his house. The lake, though, was out of sight. After he'd left me to settle in I realized with a shock that I hadn't eaten all day. No wonder I felt so weak and tired. I decided the best course of action was to get down to Hodge's shop and stock up on a few things, so I went and gave the bike another try. With a mixed feeling of relief and disappointment I discovered it still wouldn't start. I then set off walking to Millfold.

There was a little bell attached to the door of Hodge's shop. It rang as I went in, but for several minutes he pretended not to have heard. I knew he was there though. I could hear him moving about in a back room behind a sort of plastic curtain made from multi-coloured strips. It sounded as if he was brewing tea, judging by the spooning, stirring and clinking noises he was producing. Eventually I went to the door and opened it for a second time, so that the bell rang again. Only then did Hodge appear amidst the plastic strips.

'Baked beans, is it?' he asked.

'You are open then, are you?'

'Open every day,' he said. 'Early closing Wednesdays.'

'Oh, I see. Right. Yes please, baked beans.'

He went to the appropriate shelf. 'You're lucky. These are the last two cans.'

'Oh,' I said. 'You'll be getting some more in though, won't you?'

Hodge smiled in a cheery way and clapped his hands together. 'I'm afraid not.'

'Why's that?' I asked.

'No demand once the season's over. Not worth opening another box.'

'But I'll be staying for a while now, so I'll definitely be buying them.'

'That's what they all say.'

'Who?'

'People who come in here asking for things.'

'You mean customers?'

'Call them what you like,' said Hodge. 'There'll be no more beans this year.'

'So that's your final decision, is it?'

'I believe it is.'

'Oh,' I said. 'Right.'

At this point I'd liked to have walked out of the shop without buying anything at all, but unfortunately there was nowhere else to go. I had no choice but to purchase the two cans of beans plus a few other essential items, but I left determined not to give him my custom again. When I got home I remembered an advert I'd noticed in a copy of the

Trader's Gazette. It took a while to track down as there were a lot of pages and I kept being distracted by other items, but eventually I found what I was looking for.

GROCERIES DELIVERED BY VAN it said. NO ORDER TOO SMALL.

There was a local phone number, so that evening I made a list and called in at the phone box on my way to the pub. It rang about twenty times before a man answered.

'Hello.'

'Is that the van delivery service?'

'Might be,' he said. 'Who wants it?'

'Well, I'm staying in the bothy up at Mr Parker's place.'

'Oh, yes?'

'And I was wondering if I could order some groceries?'

'We go in that direction Tuesdays and Thursdays only.'

'That's OK,' I said.

'And you've got to have your order ready two days in advance.'

'Fine.'

'Alright,' he said. 'I suppose we can fit you in.'

'Thanks.'

'Wait a minute, will you? I'll just go and find something to write it down on.'

While I waited it struck me that this person had a similar approach to his customers as Hodge. I'd practically had to persuade him to deliver my groceries, and now it turned out he didn't even have a proper order book at the ready. When he eventually came back to the phone I heard him give a long, heavy sigh.

'Alright,' he said. 'Let's hear it.'

'Right,' I began. 'Er . . . sliced bread.'

There was a pause.

'Is that "sliced bread", or "er . . . sliced bread"?'

'Sliced bread.'

There was another pause as he wrote it down. 'Yes. What else?'

'Twelve cans of baked beans.'

A long pause. 'Yes. What else?'

'Tea.'

'Yes.'

'Sugar.'

'Yes.'

'Have you got any of those Fray Bentos individual cook-in-the-oven steak and kidney pies with gravy?'

'Yes, we have.'

'Three of those, please.'

He sighed again, then several seconds passed during which I could hear a pencil scribbling.

'Yes,' he said at length.

'Three pounds of potatoes.'

At this point the pips went. After I'd put another coin in there was a long silence.

'Hello?' I said.

'Hello.'

'Did you get that?'

'What?'

'Three pounds of potatoes.'

'Yes,' he said with impatience. 'What else?'

'I need some biscuits as well.'

'Yes.'

'What sort have you got?'

'All sorts.'

'Oh, right,' I said. 'Two packets of fig rolls, please.'

'No, we haven't got those.'

'How about custard creams?'

'No.'

'Malted milk?'

Now the pips went again. I put another coin in the slot and heard the same silence as before.

'Hello?' I said.

Silence.

After a long wait I hung up and redialled, but this time he didn't answer.

*　　*　　*

Over in the Packhorse they had a new consignment of Topham's Excelsior Bitter. After the frustrations of my phone call this came as welcome news, although I found it slightly surprising.

'Pint of Ex?' asked Tony, the moment I walked into the bottom bar.

'Please,' I said. 'But I thought you weren't getting any more.'

'We weren't,' he replied. 'There wasn't enough demand for it.'

'But now there is?'

'Now that you're back, yes,' he said. 'You've tipped the balance.'

'Oh well. That's good.'

Tony had already placed a glass under the tap and begun pulling the handle.

'Only thing is, we've had to mark the price up a bit.'

'Have you?'

'Just enough to cover costs.'

'How much do I owe you then?' I enquired.

He finished pulling the beer and placed a completed pint on the counter. 'This one's on the house actually.'

'Thanks,' I smiled. 'Any particular reason?'

'We want to enlist you in the darts team as a regular. We

were quite impressed by your performance the other night, and so was the visiting captain.'

'Was he?'

'She.'

'She?'

'Yes,' he said. 'You know – Lesley.'

'Oh . . . yeah, right.'

'Very impressed, she was.'

'Well, I was just lucky really. Having a good night.'

'So you're prepared to sign up with us, are you?'

'If you'd like me to, yes.'

'Of course we'd like you to.'

'Right then,' I said. 'I will.'

I had more beer than I planned to on that first night back at the Packhorse, mainly because Tony wouldn't accept any money. The first pint was 'on the house', I knew that, but when I followed it with a second, and then a third, he kept insisting that it was OK to run up a slate. I didn't want to cause offence by refusing his trust, so I went along with it and ended up having five pints. On my way home later that night I made a mental note not to allow the tally to get out of hand.

*   *   *

The first sound I heard the following morning was the 'clunk' of a milk bottle on my doorstep. Peering out of the bedroom window I saw Deakin retreating across the yard towards his truck before driving off. I thought it was a bit cheeky of him to start making deliveries without seeing me first, but I wasn't bothered really as I was going to ask him anyway. Actually I was grateful he'd woken me up, because otherwise I'd have been too late for breakfast. I got up quickly and went across to the house, where Gail let me in. She seemed quite pleased to see me.

Mr Parker was already at the table when I sat down.

'You'll be getting started on the boats today, will you?' he asked.

'Hope so,' I said. 'Of course, there'll be quite a bit of preparation to do before any paint goes on.'

'I'm glad to hear that,' he said. 'We don't want any sort of slapdash job.'

'No.'

'There's an electric sander over there in the big shed if you need it. And a blowlamp.'

'Right.'

'So you'll be able to get them done by Christmas then?'

'Oh yes. No problem.'

'Good.'

Gail placed my breakfast in front of me before sitting down herself.

'Settling into your new home alright?' continued her father.

'Yes, thanks,' I replied.

'Enough room for you?'

'Oh yes,' I said. 'Plenty.'

'That's good.'

'You're a bit like the three little pigs,' remarked Gail.

'Am I?' I asked, glancing down at my sausages.

'Yes,' she said. 'Your tent was your house of straw. Then you had a caravan, which was your house of sticks. And now you've got a house of stone.'

At that moment the Post Office van pulled up in the yard, and the driver went through the same routine as the last time I'd seen him. After bobbing up the steps he again opened the kitchen door by four inches, slipped the post onto the shelf inside, said 'Thank you', in a sing-song voice, and was gone again.

Mr Parker glanced across to the shelf. 'Ah good,' he said. 'Here's the *Gazette*.'

He stepped across the kitchen and picked up the only item of mail, a new edition of the *Trader's Gazette*, rolled up and specially labelled for postal delivery. He unwrapped it and began studying its pages with interest. In the silence that followed I remembered a question I'd been meaning to ask.

'You know those sheep?' I said.

Mr Parker looked up momentarily. 'Which sheep?'

'The ones up on the fell behind here.'

'Oh, yes.'

'Have they got anything to do with you?'

'You mean do I own them?'

'Yes.'

'No.'

'Who does then?'

'They belong to Bryan Webb mostly. He keeps his hay in our loft here.'

'Oh.'

'As a matter of fact he'll be bringing a lot of ewes through the yard sometime soon, and he may need some help directing them. I've told him you'll be around to lend a hand.'

'Oh, right,' I said. 'But you don't keep sheep yourself?'

'Not any more, no,' he replied. 'We lost a flock one winter years ago and decided to give it up.'

'That's a shame.'

'They're no longer a safe bet, sheep aren't, what with man-made fibres and everything.'

'No, suppose not.'

'So we went into buying and selling instead.'

'Yes, I noticed you do a lot of that.'

'Best way to make a living these days.'

'What about the boats?' I asked.

'What about them?'

'Aren't they a good way to make a living?'

'No,' he said. 'Practically a liability, to tell the truth.'

During this conversation Mr Parker had been going through the *Gazette* with a biro, putting marks and crosses beside certain items. Now he rose from his seat and went into the next room where the telephone was.

After he'd gone Gail said, 'What are you like at geography?'

'Well, I know east from west,' I replied. 'Why, have you got some more homework?'

She smiled. 'Yeah.'

'Alright, bring it over sometime and I'll have a look at it.'

'You can have it now if you want.' She reached under the table and produced an exercise book from her bag.

I glanced through the questions. 'OK. Should be no problem.'

'Could you get a couple wrong this time, please?' she asked.

'Why's that?'

'Well, you got twenty out of twenty for the geometry, and they might start getting suspicious.'

'Suppose so.'

'By the way,' she added. 'Your essay got read out in class.'

'Oh,' I said. 'Did it?'

'The teacher said it was the best work I'd ever done. So, thanks.'

'My pleasure.'

She smiled again and looked at the clock on the wall. 'I've got to go.'

'Yes,' I said, getting up from the table. 'I'd better get started too. Thanks for the breakfast.'

I took my leave and went across to the big shed. Someone

had already been over and undone the padlock, so I slid the
door back and went in, closing it behind me. Then I examined
the place that was going to be my workshop for the next few
weeks. Several transparent panels in the roof helped make
it quite light inside, and I noticed there were a good few
electric lamps as well. The sander and blowlamp Mr Parker
had mentioned were lying on a shelf to one side, along with
some other useful-looking equipment. Despite all the stuff
crammed into the building enough space remained between
each boat to allow plenty of room to work. There was even
a stove and chimney in one of the corners, to keep the shed
warm when the weather turned cold. All in all I was quite
encouraged by what I saw, and decided I could be quite at
home here. Before I began work I wanted to find out what
it was I'd seen glinting over at the back of the shed the first
time I came in. This meant clambering over a number of
packing cases and scaffolding tubes, and round the back of
a large metal frame that seemed to house some kind of
weighing apparatus. After a lot of squeezing through gaps I
finally saw the object of my curiosity. It was a row of motorcycles. There were half a dozen of them altogether. Some
were brand new, preserved in a layer of grease and still bearing the manufacturers' shipping labels written in Japanese.
Others were second hand, vintage models similar to mine,
and one of them even had a pre-unit gear box. I was just
wondering what Mr Parker planned to do with them all when
I heard the shed door being slid back.

Then I heard his voice. 'Where are you?'

'Over here,' I said quickly. 'I think there's a panel loose
somewhere. I was just trying to find it.'

'Oh yes,' he said. 'I heard it banging the other night. We
ought to get it fixed soon.'

He climbed over the packing cases and joined me.

'Nice bikes,' I remarked.

He nodded. 'Thought I'd hold on to them, see how the prices go.'

He was already examining the walls of the shed, searching for the loose panel. 'Looks like we need a few new rivets along here.'

I pressed at random against a corrugated sheet and it moved outwards.

'Here we are,' I said. 'The next one's a bit loose too.'

'So it is,' said Mr Parker. Then he turned to me and asked, 'Have you ever done any riveting?'

6

Three days it took me to replace all the rivets in that shed.
No sooner had Mr Parker seen the loose panels for himself than he decided this was the only suitable course of action.

'A chain is only as good as its weakest link,' he announced. 'And the same goes for rivets.'

Accordingly he produced a riveting gun and showed me how to use it. I was also given a drill to remove the old rivets, and a ladder to get at them.

'Be careful when you're up there, won't you?' he said.

I had to admit that the view from the top of the shed was spectacular. I could see a good part of the lake, as well as a long section of the road from Millfold. It gave me an idea of how much Mr Parker could observe from the front window of his house. I never seemed to get invited past the kitchen, but even there I always had the feeling of being very high up. Here on top of the shed I was higher still, so I made the most of the scenery on offer. The weather wasn't particularly pleasant though. The promise of sunshine after the rain had come to nothing, and the sky remained grey and cold. Clambering about on that ladder in the wind wasn't easy and the pace of work was very slow. Nevertheless, by the time I got towards the end of the job I had become an accomplished riveter. Occasionally Mr Parker would appear at the bottom of the ladder and ask how I was getting on, but mostly he just left me to it. Which presumably meant he was quite satisfied with what I'd done.

As we sat at breakfast on the third morning he said, 'Almost finished the shed have you?'

'Yes,' I replied. 'Just about an hour's work left to do.'

'Then you'll be able to get on with the boats?'

'Yep.'

Outside a clinking noise could be heard approaching, and next thing Deakin's pick-up truck pulled into the yard, fully laden with milk. He got out and bobbed up the steps, then ran over to the bothy before returning to the vehicle and driving off in a great hurry.

After he'd gone Mr Parker looked at me and said, 'You could do that if you wanted.'

'Sorry,' I asked. 'What?'

'The milk.'

'Oh, no,' I replied. 'I don't know a thing about cows.'

'Nor does Deakin.'

'Doesn't he?'

'Course not.'

'But I thought he was a dairyman.'

'He collects it from the dairy, yes, but that's all.'

'Oh,' I said. 'I didn't know that.'

'You'd only need a pick-up truck of your own and you could do it.'

'Well, I'd never even thought about it, really.'

'There's a good bit of business to be had in that milk round.'

'Yes, but I wouldn't want to put Deakin out of work.'

Mr Parker shook his head. 'Nobody's going to miss Deakin.'

At that moment the telephone rang in the adjoining room, instantly causing Gail to spring from her seat.

'I'll get it,' she said, darting next door.

A moment later she was back.

'Dad, it's for you.'

Mr Parker went through and picked up the receiver, while Gail sat down again opposite me.

'Homework alright, was it?' I asked.

'Yes, thanks,' she replied. 'Do you want some more?'

'Breakfast or homework?'

'Homework.'

'Yes, I don't mind doing it. What have you got?'

She reached into her bag under the table and produced a pile of exercise books.

'History, maths and comprehension.'

'Alright,' I said. 'I'll take care of it.'

Mr Parker came back into the kitchen. 'That was Bryan Webb. He's bringing his sheep through today.'

An hour later I'd finished the riveting and was just taking the ladder down when I heard them coming. There was a gateway leading from the top yard out onto the fell, beyond which I could hear someone shouting 'Ho! Ho!' again and again. Within moments the leading ewes ventured through the open gate, followed soon afterwards by the whole flock. By this time Gail had gone to school and Mr Parker was away on some business or other, which left only me to direct the sheep through the yard and down the concrete road. Having never done anything like this before I wasn't sure what to do, but I soon discovered that standing on one spot and waving my arms was the best approach. Eventually Bryan and another man appeared at the back of the nervous throng, accompanied by three efficient-looking dogs. The first thing I noticed about Bryan was that even when he was herding sheep he still wore his cardboard crown. As he passed by he took the time for a brief conversation.

'Getting on alright with that painting, are you?' he asked.

'Well I haven't got started yet,' I replied. 'Had to do some maintenance work on the shed first.'

The two men grinned at each other, and I now recognized the second one as a regular in the Packhorse.

'Well,' remarked Bryan. 'You'll have to get a move on if you're going to get it done by Christmas.'

'Should be alright.'

'And how's Tommy's temper behaving itself?'

'Oh,' I said. 'No trouble at all.'

'Really?'

'As long as I pay attention to what he says it's a piece of cake.'

'That's the secret, is it?'

'Seems to be.'

'Very good,' he said, grinning again. 'Best to keep on the right side of him.'

Soon afterwards Bryan and I said goodbye, the other man nodded, and next thing they were on their way down the hill.

Now, at last, I could get on with the boats. I'd been going in and out of the big shed continually during the last couple of days, checking new rivets, removing old ones and so forth, but I hadn't had cause to go in there this morning. Now I noticed for the first time that Mr Parker had stacked a number of paint tins just inside the door. To my dismay I discovered that they were all unlabelled, which meant the contents were green. This came as a bit of a disappointment because I'd been under the impression I was supposed to be painting the boats in their original colours. I knew he had lots of green paint, but I'd assumed that was for the workaday jobs: gates and doors and suchlike. Surely boats with classical prows deserved something slightly better. That's what I'd have thought anyway. Nonetheless, there was plenty of preparation to do before I even opened a tin of paint, so I set my disappointment aside and got started with the electric sander.

It didn't take long to come to the conclusion that whoever

painted the boats in the first place had done a very thorough job. Maybe paint was of a better quality in those days, but this stuff almost seemed to be impregnated into the timber. Only by concentrating hard did I make any impression on it at all. Hour after hour I worked with that sander, head down, battling against layer upon layer of stubborn paint and making very slow progress. It was a noisy operation, and for this reason I failed to hear the arrival of a vehicle in the yard outside. Only when the shed door opened did I realize I had a visitor. It was Deakin.

He came inside and I switched off the sander.

'Oh,' he said, as the noise faded away. 'Tommy's got you doing this, has he?'

'Yeah,' I replied. 'Did you want him?'

'Yes, I could do with having a word with him about something.'

'Well, you've missed him again. Why don't you speak to him when you bring the milk?'

'No time,' he said. 'It's alright, I'll come back another day.'

'It's not urgent then?'

'Not really, no.'

He made no move to leave, but instead stood peering around the inside of the shed. After a while his eyes fell on the space occupied by my motorbike.

'Ah,' he said. 'I see he's got rid of the snow plough at last.'

'Er . . . oh, yes,' I said. 'It went the other day.'

'Been in here since we built the shed, that has.'

'Did you help him build it then?'

'Yes,' he said, with a note of pride. 'It was me who did all the riveting.'

Soon afterwards he wandered off. I watched him slide open the door and close it behind him. Then I started up the sander again. A few moments later another sound came floating into the shed from outside. I switched off just in time to hear the unmistakable chimes of an ice-cream van. They were playing 'Half a pound of treacle'.

Quickly I went to the door and looked out, but the yard was completely empty.

*   *   *

Mr Parker returned that evening with some more oil drums. I was just finishing work for the day when he pulled into the top yard in his pick-up, so I went to lend him a hand unloading them. The group of drums by the gateway now numbered something like fifty, but he seemed determined to bring back even more every time he went out. This time there were half a dozen on the trailer, and another four in the rear of the pick-up.

A little later I went into the bothy for a cup of tea. The door was permanently unlocked, and as soon as I entered I realized there'd been another caller that afternoon apart from Deakin. Just inside the doorway someone had left a box containing my grocery order. I went through the items one by one and discovered that everything I'd asked for was there, apart from the biscuits, which were the wrong type. They'd evidently decided that since there were no fig rolls, custard creams or malted milks, I would have to make do with plain digestives instead. Attached to the box was an invoice for the order. It bore a message, written across the bottom in red pencil: *'No more beans after this.'*

There was also one large printed word at the head of the invoice: 'HODGE'. I put the groceries away and lit the kettle.

That night in the Packhorse I played my first Inter-Pub League darts match as a full team member. We had an away game against the Journeyman coming up which I was quite looking forward to, but in the meantime we were facing the Golden Lion at home. It was the usual sort of turnout, with Bryan Webb captaining us to victory once again. The visiting team had no women supporters travelling with them, though, so the evening had a bit of a flat edge to it from that point of view. My opponent from the Golden Lion was a portly bloke called Phil who didn't seem the slightest bit bothered when I beat him, and instantly rushed off to buy me a pint of lager. When I asked if it would be alright if I had Topham's Excelsior instead he looked slightly sorry for me, as though I hadn't been properly weaned or something.

'Better put him a spare one in the pump as well,' he said to Tony.

'Oh,' I said. 'Thanks very much. Cheers.'

These darts people certainly were a friendly crowd, and made up for the shortage of women by buying each other lots of drinks. I always seemed to be on the receiving end, but even when I ordered a round of my own I didn't have to pay. Tony was doubling as vice-captain and barman, and repeatedly gave this as the reason to continue my slate for the time being.

'You can settle up when we're less busy,' he kept saying, before returning to the oche for another game.

'Yes, alright,' I replied. 'But I must pay you what I owe you soon.'

'Don't worry about it,' he said with a grin.

I judged from my treatment by the locals that they all knew I would be staying around for the foreseeable future. I was already aware that everyone knew everybody else's business round here, and this was confirmed time and again as the days passed. Kenneth Turner, for example, kept saying that he would have to come and have a look at my bike sometime, while Bryan Webb was forever enquiring about my progress with the boats. And there was always some new story about Deakin delivering the wrong milk, or arriving too late.

At the end of one such account Bryan turned to me and said, 'You ought to take over from Deakin.'

I wasn't sure whether this remark was meant to be treated seriously or not, but as he said it a definite murmur of assent went round the bottom bar.

*   *   *

A few evenings later as I crossed the yard on my way to the pub, I became aware of a rhythmic thumping noise inside the big shed. It was about nine o'clock and the electric lights had all been switched on, so I went over and peered through the doorway, which was open by about one inch. I saw straight away that the thumping noise was coming from the concrete mixer. Its diesel engine had been put back together and started up, and it was now being watched intently by Mr Parker and Kenneth Turner. Kenneth was wearing a blue boiler suit and stood holding an adjustable spanner in his hand. Both of them seemed to be mesmerized by the mixer's bucket, which rotated slowly round and round before their eyes. For a whole minute they looked at it, then another minute after that, while I stood outside in the dark, watching them. Eventually Mr Parker said something and Kenneth nodded. He dropped the spanner into a deep pocket and they walked over towards my motorbike. Next moment Kenneth was astride it and kicking the engine over. To my surprise it roared into life, and he spent some time revving it up and listening to it closely, while the concrete mixer continued to throb away unattended. Eventually Kenneth cut the bike engine again, and he and Mr Parker stood examining the paintwork and the chrome. Then they turned and had a look at the boat I'd been working on during the day. Kenneth picked up one of the tins of paint that were still waiting unopened nearby. When he saw it had no label he grinned broadly at Mr Parker. Then the two of them clambered over the packing cases in the direction of the other motorcycles at the back of the shed. At this point I tired of spying on them and continued on my way down the yard. Glancing at the house I realized that Gail must have been on her own inside, and casually I wondered what she did during the evenings now she had no homework to occupy her.

With a sudden shock I remembered I had some grammar to hand in by tomorrow morning! I'd been having a bath for the last hour and gone and forgotten all about it! Now I had to rush back to the bothy and get it done before I could go out. It seemed to take longer than usual, and as a result I didn't get going to the pub again until almost ten, by which time the big shed was in complete darkness. When I arrived at the Packhorse I saw Kenneth sitting on his usual stool at the end of the counter. He said, 'Hello,' but didn't mention his visit to Mr Parker's place, so I didn't mention it either.

Next morning I was woken up by the rhythmic thumping again. Looking through the curtains I saw that Mr Parker was already up and about. He'd opened the shed doors wide and hauled the concrete mixer outside onto the loading bay. It stood there with the engine running, and the bucket going round and round. After a while I saw him look at his watch and then peer in the direction of the bothy. I took this as a signal that it was time to get up, so I heaved myself out of bed. Something told me I wouldn't be getting much work done on the boats today, but he didn't reveal his plans until we were sitting having breakfast.

'It's about time we made a new mooring weight for the boats,' he announced. 'If we leave it any longer the lake'll be too rough.'

'Gets bad in the winter, does it?' I asked.

'Can do,' he said. 'And there's no point in putting the job off until spring.'

'No, spose not.'

'You know how to make a mooring weight, do you?'

'Got a rough idea, yeah.'

'That's good. I've got all the tackle ready for you. There's a lorry wheel, some long chain and plenty of concrete.'

'Right.'

'All you've got to do is mix it.'

'OK.'

A few moments passed. Across the yard the rhythmic thumping continued.

'Did you get that homework done?' asked Gail.

'Oh yes,' I replied. 'Forgot to bring it over. It's all finished, you can collect it when you want.'

'Thanks,' she said. 'By the way, your essay won a prize.'

'Did it?'

'Yeah, they printed it in the school magazine.'

'Well,' I said. 'I'm quite pleased about that really. What was the prize?'

'A book token.'

'Oh, that's good.'

'Do you want it?'

'Don't *you* want it?'

'Not really.'

'Oh, OK then.'

'You can have it as a reward for doing all that homework.'

'Er . . . thanks.'

She reached down into her school bag and produced the book token, placing it on the table.

'You'd better sign that on the back,' remarked her father.

I thought he was making a joke, but next thing Gail had a biro in her hand and was solemnly writing her signature.

'Thanks,' I said again as she handed me the token. 'Have you got a copy of the magazine so I can see myself in print?'

'Oh no, sorry,' she replied. 'I threw it away.'

A clinking noise outside heralded the arrival of Deakin's pick-up. We watched through the window as he rushed about making his hurried deliveries, first to the house, then to the bothy, before quickly departing.

'I gather they're on strike again in the south,' said Mr Parker.

'Oh, are they?' I said. 'I hadn't heard.'

'It was on the television last night.'

'Have you got a television then?'

'Yes, of course. Why?'

'Well, I just didn't think people round here bothered with televisions. What with the scenery and everything.'

'Oh yes, we have one through there,' he said, nodding towards the next room. 'Got it for *One Man and His Dog*.'

'What are they on strike about?' asked Gail. She was looking at me.

'They're probably worried about unemployment,' I suggested.

'So how does going on strike help?'

'Er . . . well, it doesn't really,' I said. 'It's supposed to be a sort of statement.'

'Oh,' she said. 'I see.'

'I don't believe in unemployment,' said Mr Parker.

'Don't you?'

'No such thing. There's always something to do.'

'Spose.'

'Did they have many strikes at that factory of yours?'

'Not while I was there, no.'

'Sounds like an efficient little operation.'

'Yes, it seemed to be doing very well.'

'Pay good wages?'

'Not bad.'

'Get plenty saved up, did you?'

'A bit, yes.'

'That's good.'

The way the conversation was going it struck me as an appropriate time to bring up a matter I'd been avoiding for the last week or so. The problem was that when I'd agreed to work on the boats we'd failed to discuss how much I was going to get paid. I had no idea if I was supposed to be getting a fixed sum for the job, or an hourly rate, or what, so I decided to broach the subject now.

'Er . . . actually,' I said, 'while we're on the subject of work . . .'

'You're quite right,' said Mr Parker, rising abruptly to his feet. 'We're not going to get anything done by sitting here.'

Next thing he was heading for the kitchen door, and I had no choice but hurriedly to finish my breakfast and follow.

We went outside and crossed the yard to the mixer, which was still rotating its empty bucket round and round. Beside it was a barrow containing the ingredients for the concrete. Also a wheel hub and a huge length of galvanized chain. It was too noisy by the mixer to pursue the question of my wages, so I gave up for the time being. Besides, there was no real urgency as I hadn't been required to part with any money for some time now. I was still running a slate at the Pack-horse, while all my groceries and milk were being delivered on credit. Obviously these concurrent debts would have to be sorted out in the near future, but nobody seemed in much of a hurry to collect, so I decided not to worry about it.

Making up the mooring weight was quite straightforward. I attached one end of the chain to the wheel hub, and then began shovelling sand, gravel and cement into the mixer. As soon as he was satisfied that I knew what I was doing, Mr Parker said he would 'leave me to it', and set off somewhere in his pick-up with the trailer in tow. Shortly afterwards Gail headed down the hill in her school uniform, giving me her usual little wave. When the concrete was ready I poured it into the wheel hub, and left it to set. I reckoned it would need a week to cure before it could be safely dropped to the bottom of the lake.

This task hadn't taken very long at all, and the result looked OK. Before I resumed work on the boats I decided to reward myself with a cup of tea, and wandered over to the bothy. Lying on the table was the latest copy of the *Trader's Gazette*. I'd got into the habit of borrowing it after Mr Parker had gleaned all the information he required. This was simply out of interest and curiosity, as I had no intention of buying any of the items advertised inside. I made a mental note that now I had a book token I really should get myself something proper to read, but in the meantime I opened the *Gazette* at a random page. There my eyes fell on an advertisement I hadn't seen before. It was listed under 'Services' in the Millfold area and said:

CIRCULAR SAW WITH MAN FOR HIRE
All timber-cutting work undertaken on site.
Enquiries T. Parker

A telephone number was also given. I read the advert several times to make sure I wasn't mistaken, then continued turning the pages. Further along someone was inviting advance orders for Christmas trees. Ten per cent discount would be given for immediate payment. This struck me as a bit early until it occurred to me that Christmas was now only a couple of months away. Autumn had certainly crept up on me as I laboured away at my boats, and a blast of wind outside confirmed this. I'd hardly noticed that the weather was slowly worsening because I spent a good part of each day in the big shed. Even so, the signs were obvious. Despite all the riveting I'd done, the shed continued to creak and groan as the elements pounded against it. There were other indications too. The trees were bare, and the temperature was declining slowly. When I walked to the pub at night I could hear seabirds out in the middle of the lake, squawking and arguing. It sounded as though there were thousands of them. I had no idea where they'd come from, but they seemed to have settled in for the winter. I thought about the seven boats waiting to be painted, the darts fixtures and the endless pints of Topham's Excelsior Bitter, and realized that I'd settled in for the winter as well.

*   *   *

It was almost dark when Mr Parker returned with yet another load of oil drums.

Having just finished work for the evening, I went out into the yard to meet him. There was something I wanted to ask him about the mooring weight.

'It's quite heavy,' I said. 'How are we going to get it out onto the lake?'

'You're the boat man,' he replied. 'You tell me.'

'Well, if we use the tender it'll tip straight over.'

'Will it?'

'Yeah. We need a proper mooring raft really, with a hole in the middle to drop the weight through.'

'Oh,' he said. 'I see.'

When Mr Parker first told me he knew nothing about boats I hadn't really taken him seriously, but over the past few weeks I'd come to realize it was true. He didn't seem to have any idea about how to lay a mooring, and I now saw that I was going to have to take charge of the operation.

'So how do we make a mooring raft?' he asked.

'Quite easily,' I replied. 'It just takes four empty oil drums and some planks.'

'Well I can't spare any oil drums.'

'Oh . . . can't you?'

'Not really,' he said. 'I wanted to sell them all to that factory of yours.'

'Is that why you've been collecting them?'

'Of course it is. You told me I'd get a good price.'

'Yeah, but . . . it's miles away.'

'That's alright. I don't mind how far I have to go as long as I make a profit.'

'How will you get them all there though?'

'On my lorry.'

'I didn't know you had one.'

'Yes, you've seen it. Over in Bryan Webb's barn.'

'Oh, right.'

'He keeps his hay here, I keep my lorry there.'

'Sounds like a handy arrangement.'

'It's mutually beneficial and saves exchanging cash.'

I nodded and we fell silent. Mr Parker gazed at the mooring weight and appeared to be pondering my suggestion.

'Well,' he said at length. 'I suppose I could set aside four drums at a push. Can you build this raft?'

'Can if you like, yes.'

'OK then,' he said. 'The job's yours.'

*   *   *

As usual in the evening I treated myself to a bath. This was probably the best thing about staying in the bothy. There was plenty of hot water, and although the bath took a long time to fill, it was always a luxurious moment at the end of a hard day. I generally waited until after I'd taken my evening meal, and then spent an hour or so wallowing before going out to the pub. Tonight was no exception. Round about eight o'clock I began running the taps and slowly the bathroom filled with steam. Ten minutes later I slid into the hot water, easing myself down until it lapped over me. How long I'd been lying there before I was interrupted I wasn't sure. I had my ears below the surface and my feet up on the sides of the bath when I became aware of a knocking noise. For a moment I thought it was a loose panel on the shed, but then I remembered it couldn't have been that. No, this noise was coming from somewhere much closer. I sat up and listened again. Someone was tapping the window from outside. Leaving the bath I went over and peered through the frosted glass. I could just make out a pink oval in the darkness.

'Hello?'

It was Gail.

'We've just had the Packhorse on the phone,' she said. 'You're supposed to be at darts.'

'But it's the wrong night,' I said.

'That's the message,' she replied, and the pink oval was gone.

Wondering how much she'd seen through the glass, I quickly got dried and dressed. The message made no sense at all. Every darts match up until now had been on a Thursday. Today was only Tuesday, so I had no idea what they wanted me for. Surely they wouldn't ring up just to get me to a practice session? It was only a game, after all. Still, I thought I'd better get going right away, so I went across to the big shed to get my bike out. Finding that Mr Parker had

locked it up for the night, I decided to walk instead. I'd long
come to the conclusion that this was more sensible anyway,
judging by the amount of beer that flowed at these darts
nights. In the event, though, it probably would have been
better to take the bike.

The moment I walked into the bottom bar I knew something was wrong. It was half past nine and the place should
have been packed out on a darts night. Instead it was almost
deserted. There was no sign of Tony or Gordon. The landlord
was talking to one or two people in the top bar and took no
notice of me for some time. When at last he did decide to
serve me he was far from friendly.

'Yes?' he said.

'Where is everybody?' I asked.

'They're playing at the Journeyman,' he replied. 'Where
you're supposed to be.'

'But I thought darts was on Thursdays.'

'That's home games!' he snapped. 'Away matches are
Tuesdays.'

'Oh,' I said. 'I didn't know that.'

'Don't you ever read the fixture list?'

'Er . . . no, sorry.'

'Well, you're too late now. The match'll be half over.'

'Sorry.'

'What do you want?'

'Pint of Ex, please.'

'Barrel's finished.'

'Oh.' I said. 'Well, I don't mind waiting while you change
it.'

'I'm not going to change it.'

'Aren't you?'

'No, I'm afraid not.'

And with that he returned to the top bar, where his cronies
all seemed to be glaring down at me. I remained standing

there feeling awkward and wondering what to do, when I noticed that I wasn't quite alone. Also present in the bottom bar was Bryan Webb's accomplice from the sheep-moving day. Since that occasion we'd become slightly better acquainted, and I now knew that his name was Maurice. Apparently he was the man who drove the school minibus. He beckoned me to join him, so I went over and he spoke quietly.

'Understandable mistake,' he said. 'Couldn't be helped.'

'No,' I said. 'I'd have come earlier if I'd known. I've been looking forward to playing the Journeyman again.'

'I know you have, but you've gone and upset them all now, so you'll have to keep your head down for a while.'

'What shall I do then?'

'Well, your best bet is to drink somewhere else for a week or two, until they've forgotten all about it.'

I felt a sudden surge of dismay.

'But there's only the Ring of Bells,' I said.

Maurice looked at me with sympathy. 'That's it then, isn't it?'

7

The following afternoon I was working inside the shed when 'Half a pound of treacle' came floating in from the yard. Quickly I went over and peered through the crack in the door just as a yellow and white ice-cream van pulled up outside. It was a very traditional sort of vehicle. There was a large plastic cornet mounted on the roof, below which were written the words 'SNAITHES OF WAINSKILL' in blue letters. The vehicle came to a halt with its refrigerator unit whirring away, and all its lights blazing. For a few moments I couldn't see the driver, whose head was hidden as he fiddled about underneath the dashboard. He seemed to be having considerable trouble with the chimes, which kept repeating 'Half a pound of treacle' at random, and over which he apparently had no control. They were quite loud too. The sound emanated from four silver horns at the front of the vehicle before echoing off the various buildings around the yard. I slid the shed door open and went outside. Looking into the cab I could see that the driver was desperately trying to relocate various wires in an attempt to influence the chimes, but to little effect. I knocked on the window and he glanced round. It was Deakin.

'These damn chimes,' he said, sliding across the driving seat and climbing out. 'They keep getting stuck.'

'Can't you turn them off altogether?' I suggested.

'No,' he replied. 'If I do that the headlights go out and the refrigerator stops working.'

'Oh dear.'

'It's all wired up wrong and I can never get it sorted out.'

'What happened to the rest of the tune then?'

'Don't know,' he said. 'I've never heard anything except "Half a pound of treacle".'

While we talked we were being constantly interrupted by blasts from the quadruple horns, and on each occasion we had to break off our conversation until the din subsided.

'Would you like me to have a look at it?' I asked.

'Can if you like,' he said. 'I'm at the end of my tether. Tommy's not here, I suppose?'

'No, sorry.'

I got into the cab and discovered that it was just as noisy in there, what with the refrigerator unit throbbing away and the chimes sounding repeatedly overhead. There was a control switch on the dashboard, below which a number of coloured wires protruded. I tried swapping some of them around, but only succeeded in making the lights inside the plastic cornet start flashing on and off. I put the wires back how I'd found them and got out. Then I proposed that we went into the shed for a bit of peace and quiet.

'Your name's not Snaithe, is it?' I enquired when we got inside.

'No,' he said. 'It's Deakin.'

'That's what I thought. So who's Snaithe then?'

'He's the man who owned the ice-cream factory at Wainskill.'

'Oh,' I said. 'I didn't know there was one there.'

'Well he's been bought out by the wholesalers now, but they kept the name.'

'So how come you're driving that van then?'

Deakin shook his head. 'Don't even ask.'

'Oh, OK.'

'Well, I'll tell you if you want.' He glanced round at the

upturned boats, and sat down on the nearest one before continuing. 'That ice-cream van used to come here during holiday time and do good business. There was always a queue of campers wanting cornets and wafers. And lollies. Bit of a gold mine, it was. When Snaithe sold up he kept the franchise separate and offered it to Tommy with the van included. Tommy snapped it up, of course, but then he persuaded me to take it over.'

'But you're too busy doing your milk round, aren't you?'

'That's what I told him, but he insisted I could do the ice-cream as well, in my spare time.'

At that moment Deakin was interrupted from outside by a chorus of 'Half a pound of treacle'.

'Why didn't you just say no?' I asked, when it was over.

Deakin sighed and shook his head again. 'Tommy made it sound like a good idea. I ended up trading in my lorry for the pick-up and the van.'

'Is that the lorry over at Bryan Webb's?'

'That's the one.'

'Any cash involved?'

'No, it was a mutually beneficial agreement. But that's what I want to see Tommy about. I was only supposed to be taking the van on trial, but I seem to be stuck with it now.'

'Didn't you like selling ice-creams then?'

'It was so busy I was worn to a frazzle!' said Deakin. 'Then the season ended and it went dead.'

'Yes, I suppose it would.'

'So I've decided against it. The van's no use for anything else and I want to give it back.'

'Well, why don't you?'

''Cos I can never catch Tommy.'

An air of gloom and despondency had begun to descend upon Deakin. He sat on the boat rubbing the palms of his hands over the sanded-down paintwork in an agitated manner. As a result they gradually turned maroon. When he noticed this a look of dismay crossed his face, and I had to resist an urge to put my arm round his shoulder and say, 'There, there.'

Instead, I offered him a cloth to wipe his hands on, followed by tea and biscuits in the bothy.

'If you take my advice,' I said, while we waited for the kettle to boil, 'you'll have a word with Tommy next time you see him.'

'Yes,' said Deakin. 'I must come and get it sorted out.'

'Don't put it off any longer than necessary.'

'No, you're right.'

'By the way, I ought to settle up with you for my milk.'

'Don't worry about that,' he said. 'There's plenty of time.'

Now that he'd got the matter of the ice-cream van off his chest Deakin seemed to perk up a bit. By the time I'd served him a cup of tea with some biscuits he was beginning to return to normal. Then his eyes fell on the new copy of the *Trader's Gazette*.

'Ooh yes,' he said. 'There's something in here I must show you.'

He reached over and began leafing through until he found the page he wanted. It came as no surprise when he showed me the item advertising 'CIRCULAR SAW WITH MAN FOR HIRE'.

'That's you,' he announced.

'Yes,' I replied. 'I thought it must be.'

'Hasn't Tommy mentioned it then?'

'Not directly, no.'

'Well,' said Deakin. 'He hires you out for so much an hour, and pays you so much an hour, and the difference is his profit.'

'Does that include wear and tear?'

'Er . . . no. Wear and tear would be a separate calculation.'

'Oh, right,' I said. 'Have you any idea what his hourly rate is?'

'No, sorry.'

'Well, what did he pay you?'

'When?'

'When you helped him build the shed.'

'Nothing.'

'What!'

'The thing is,' he said, 'Tommy doesn't like parting with cash. Not if he can help it.'

'No, I've noticed.'

'But I dare say I got something or other for my trouble.'

'You mean payment in kind?'

'Sort of, yes.' Deakin rose to his feet. 'Anyway, thanks for the tea and biscuits, but I must get a move on. I've got some homogenized milk in the refrigerator. Special delivery.'

'Where to?'

'It's for Bryan Webb's Uncle Rupert. He's always there on Wednesdays.'

Not long after that Deakin was on his way. I went out into the yard and stood watching as he descended the concrete road in his surplus ice-cream van. Then I heard the clarion call of 'Half a pound of treacle', and he was gone.

*   *   *

That night I began my two-week sentence at the Ring of Bells. Two weeks of sitting in a pub with no women, no darts and no Topham's Excelsior Bitter wasn't very appealing, so I put it off until about quarter to ten. Prior to that I passed a couple of hours drawing up plans for the mooring raft and wondering why I'd talked myself into building the thing. The truth was that although I knew what it was supposed to look like, I had no actual experience of putting one together. Only after I'd messed about with a pencil and paper for half the evening did I come up with a suitable 'design'. Then, when I'd run out of things to do, I went out.

The Ring of Bells seemed even quieter now than it had done during my previous visit. The same people sat in the same places and stared at their drinks, while the landlord (whose name, apparently, was Cyril) stood behind the counter and polished glasses. The conversation was at best desultory. Occasionally someone would make a remark about the weather, or mention whom they'd seen during the day, but most of the talk was less interesting than that. Hodge was present, of course, occupying one of the stools near the counter. He nodded when I walked in and I nodded back, and it struck me, not for the first time, that our relationship was an odd one. I'd been regularly phoning in with my grocery orders for quite a while now, and receiving invoices which I hadn't paid yet. I was sure it was Hodge who answered when I rang, but he never acknowledged the fact and I never identified myself either. I just asked for the groceries to be delivered to the bothy. If Hodge knew it was me, then he didn't let on. For my part, I had no idea when I was supposed to settle the invoice. Nothing was ever said, and we just sat side by side drinking and having little to do with one another.

Not until the third such evening did the subject of groceries come under discussion, and even then it was only brief. Hodge turned to me at the end of a particularly quiet interlude and said, 'By the way, we've got a new consignment of beans at the shop.'

'Baked beans?'

'Yes.'

'Oh, right,' I said. 'I'll bear it in mind.'

'Just thought I'd let you know.'

'Thanks.'

After that we both returned to contemplating our drinks, and the matter wasn't raised again.

Walking home it occurred to me that I could have gone over to the Journeyman to see if Lesley was around. After all, she'd been very friendly on that first night we played darts together, offering to buy me a drink and then saying, 'Maybe another time.' This had seemed like a very obvious hint. The only trouble was that I didn't have a good enough 'excuse' for suddenly turning up at her local. Wainskill was a good ten miles away and the road went there specially, so I could hardly walk in and say that I just happened to be passing through. The darts match I'd missed would have provided the perfect opportunity to get to know her better, but unfortunately this chance had gone. Now I had no idea when I would see her again.

*   *   *

Meanwhile, I spent my days trying to get on with the boats, only for the work repeatedly to be postponed by Mr Parker. It seemed there was always something else cropping up that was more urgent. One morning, soon after I'd agreed to build the mooring raft, he announced that all the materials I required were waiting for me down by the jetty.

'Do you want to get started on it today?' he asked.

'Could do,' I replied. 'Of course, it means I'll have to abandon the work on the boats for the time being.'

'That's alright,' he said. 'Christmas is still weeks away.'

His word was my command, so a little later I found myself amidst a collection of oil drums and planks. There was also a box of coach bolts to hold everything together. Assembling these components into a complete unit took a lot of trial and error, despite my carefully drawn 'plan', and the work took all day. The finished raft looked fairly robust, but whether it would float or not was a different matter. I tried hauling it to the water's edge for a buoyancy test and discovered it was quite heavy. In fact, I could only move it with the greatest difficulty. This was something I hadn't thought of. I was struggling with some spare planks trying to make a sort of slipway when someone came up behind me and said, 'Need a hand there?'

It was the old man who'd helped me repair the jetty.

'Oh thanks,' I said. 'Yes, two of us should be able to get it launched.'

'You built this, did you?' he asked, examining the raft.

'Yeah, just finished it.'

'Wouldn't have caught that other lad making anything like this.'

'No?'

'Never. Just lounged about all day long, playing with the girls.'

'What girls?'

'All of them,' he said. 'Holidaymakers, day-trippers. Didn't do a stroke apart from pulling them in with his boathook.'

'Sounds like nice work,' I remarked.

'Work?' snapped the old man. 'That's not work!' He walked round the other side of the raft and found a suitable hand-hold. 'Well, do you want a lift with this or not?'

'Yes, please,' I said. 'That'd be a great help.'

I grabbed the raft on my side and the two of us succeeded in dragging it to the water's edge. Another pull and it was floating beside the jetty. Then I tied it up and tried walking about on the deck.

'Stable, is it?' he asked.

'Seems alright,' I replied. 'Yes, I'm quite pleased.'

I came ashore and began tidying up the remaining gear.

'You've done a good job there,' he said.

'Thanks.'

'I hear you're working at our place tomorrow.'

'Am I?'

'With the circular saw.'

'Oh,' I said. 'Er . . . yeah, right.'

'Eight o'clock, you're coming.'

'OK.'

Obviously Mr Parker's advertisement in the *Trader's Gazette* had brought some response, but this was the first I'd heard of it. No doubt he planned to tell me about it in his own good time. Meanwhile, I was struck by the thought that I always seemed to be the last to find out about anything round here. Even the old man knew before I did.

'Where is it you live again?' I asked.

'Stonecroft,' he said, pointing along the lake. 'Second turning on the left.'

'Righto.'

'About time we got all that timber cut.'

'Yes.'

'Six months it's been lying there.'

'Well,' I said. 'Should be able to get a start on it tomorrow.'

He nodded and wandered off into the trees without saying goodbye. I carried on tidying up, and shortly afterwards Mr Parker arrived in his pick-up.

'Finished then?' he asked, as he got out.

'Yes,' I replied. 'Do you want to test it?'

'Could do, I suppose.' He walked onto the jetty and made as if to step onto the floating raft, but then seemed to change his mind. 'No, I'll take your word for it.'

'It's quite safe,' I said.

'Quite probably,' he replied. 'But there's no point in taking unnecessary risks.'

'No, suppose not.'

I loaded the remaining equipment into the back of Mr Parker's pick-up, and then waited as he surveyed my handiwork.

'By the way,' he said at length. 'I'll be taking you off the boats again tomorrow, if you don't mind.'

'Oh, OK. Why's that then?'

'We've got a hire contract for the circular saw, up at Pickthall's. It'll be a day's work cutting firewood.'

'Right.'

'Mr Pickthall wants you there at eight o'clock. Make sure you do a proper job for him, won't you?'

'I'll try my best.'

'That's good.'

It was almost dark now, so we got into the truck and drove up to the yard. Entering the bothy I noticed immediately that Gail had been in and taken the history homework I'd left on the shelf inside the door. In its place she'd deposited her geometry book, along with a note saying the latest exercises had to be handed in the day after tomorrow. It occurred to me that Gail was starting to take advantage of my good intentions. I didn't mind doing the homework as it was quite easy and gave me something to do after dark. There was even something to learn from it. I'd discovered over the past few weeks, for example, that her geography teacher was very interested in limestone. Questions about stalactites, stalagmites and swallow holes cropped up regularly, and any answers which included the words 'sediment' and 'precipitation' were sure to receive favourable marks. Meanwhile, the English teacher had a fascination with the concept of irony. Questions about the ironic condition seemed to be his or her stock-in-trade. I only had to suggest in an essay that such-and-such a fictional character seemed to be mocked by fate or circumstance, and I'd be rewarded with a red star and 'v.g.' beneath my final paragraph.

Nevertheless, I was slowly beginning to recognize that Gail did much better out of the arrangement than me. After all, she only had to present the latest batch of homework at the bothy and it was completed at the drop of a hat, which left her free every evening to do whatever she liked. The least she could have done in return was bring it over while I was at home. On the other hand, I had to admit I sometimes found it hard to concentrate when she was present. The homework always took twice as long if she was sitting on the sofa waiting for me to finish it off, so maybe delivering it in my absence was just her way of being considerate.

I glanced casually through the geometry exercises, which all seemed fairly straightforward. Gail had already answered one of them herself, and I was quite pleased to see that she'd got it right, apart from spelling hypotenuse incorrectly.

*　　*　　*

There was no sign of Mr Parker when I arose next morning, but the doors of the big shed had been left open and the tractor and circular saw were all ready to go. I felt quite professional when I arrived at Stonecroft at eight o'clock on the dot. The place was completely different to Hillhouse in that it was sited very low down at the foot of steeply rising ground. Access was by means of a long deep lane running between two hedgerows, and I would never have found the entrance if the old man hadn't told me it was the second on the left. After a quarter of a mile or so the lane ended in a farmyard, above which loomed a towering fell. As expected, the house was made entirely of stone. I must have got used to being high up at Mr Parker's, because this place seemed really low down and hemmed in. Also very damp. It was a gloomy day, but I couldn't imagine the sun shining much here even in the summer. There was a lot of bare rock round about, much of it covered with a mossy sheen as though it never dried out properly. And, of course, the lake was completely lost from view, the only thing to see being the grassy slopes that soared up into the clouds.

The man who emerged from the house to meet me showed signs of having lived in the shade all his life. There I was arriving fully equipped to do some important work for him, and all he did was point glumly to a stack of timber at the far side of the yard. He then looked at his watch to check that I'd turned up on time. Despite this lacklustre greeting, however, I decided to try a bit of friendly chat. Switching the engine off, I got down from the tractor.

'Morning,' I said in a cheery way. 'Mr Pickthall, is it?'

'That's right, yes,' he replied.

'Oh . . . er, well, I've brought the saw.'

'Yes, I can see that,' he said. 'And you're the operator are you?'

'Yep.'

'Right. Well, I want logs for firewood no less than nine inches and no more than fourteen. Got that?'

'No more than nine and no less than fourteen. OK.'

Mr Pickthall gave me a funny look when I said this. He glanced at the machinery and then back at me. 'You do know what you're doing, do you?'

'Oh yes,' I said, with a reassuring nod.

'Right, well, it's ten past eight so you'd better get started.'

Obviously I didn't look as professional as I thought. I started the tractor again and set the circular saw into operation, aware that Mr Pickthall was watching my every move. After doing a couple of important-looking safety checks I chose a piece of timber from the stack and began cutting it into chunks. Each one looked as if it was between nine and fourteen inches to me, but after a while he produced a tape from his pocket and took a measurement. Then he came over to the tractor.

'Haven't you got a yardstick?' he demanded.

'Er . . . well, no,' I replied. 'Don't usually bother with one.'

'So you're just guessing the lengths, are you?'

'Yeah.'

He shook his head. 'Well, I haven't got time to stay here any longer, but there had better not be any mistakes.'

'OK.'

'Otherwise Mr Parker'll hear about it.'

'Right.'

And with that he went back into the house and closed the door. A few minutes later he came out again, glanced towards me, and then headed for a low-roofed shed inside which was parked a pick-up truck. I felt quite relieved when he got in and drove away up the lane without a further word. As soon as he'd gone I switched off and stopped for a rest. I'd begun work so quickly after arriving that I'd barely had a chance to look at the place, so now I stood peering around for a few minutes. The first thing I noticed was that the house seemed to be divided into two parts. The door Mr Pickthall had used was nearest to me, and on the step was an empty milk bottle. At the far end of the building I now saw another doorstep with a milk bottle of its own. For a moment I thought I caught sight of a pink face in the window, peeping out, but there was no time for further observation. Suddenly I heard a vehicle coming along the lane, and thinking it was Mr Pickthall returning I started up and got back to work.

A moment later Deakin arrived in the yard.

As usual he was in a great hurry, running to the two doorsteps with fresh milk and retrieving the empty bottles. When he noticed me standing by the tractor he gave me a frantic wave.

'Seen Tommy yet?' I called.

'No!' he replied. 'Haven't had time! But I will!'

'Well, make sure you do!'

'Alright!'

Next thing Deakin was gone, charging off down the lane to continue his milk round, which was beginning to look like a very thankless task. Why everybody round here thought I'd be interested in 'taking over' was beyond me. Even Hodge seemed to have picked up the idea from somewhere. The previous evening in the Ring of Bells he'd started going on about there being 'room for improvement in the milk business', and how a good candidate 'wasn't a million miles away'. I'd pretended to take no notice of all this, of course, and didn't engage in any direct conversation with him. Nevertheless, I got the strong impression that several people were convinced I seriously was considering being their milk-man. As far as I knew I'd done nothing to substantiate this belief, and the last thing I wanted to do was usurp Deakin. He had enough troubles already without me adding to them.

With these thoughts in mind I returned to the circular saw and continued work. Shortly afterwards I noticed someone emerging from the far end of the house. It was the old man. He was wearing some heavy-duty gloves and work boots, and heading straight in my direction. In his hand was some sort of stick. As he crossed the yard he glanced at the near end of the house from time to time, and also at the shed where the pick-up had been parked. Finally he joined me and waved the stick.

'Measuring rod,' he said by way of greeting. 'Don't expect you've got one, have you?'

'No,' I replied. 'Thanks.'

'What's he told you? Nine to fourteen?'

'Yes.'

'Thought so. Alright, carry on.'

Next thing he was dragging a huge length of timber towards the saw. Then he went along with the measuring rod marking off lengths for cutting. As usual his presence speeded up the operation appreciably, and in the next hour I got a good deal of work done. Mr Pickthall hadn't mentioned it, but the completed logs were apparently supposed to be deposited in a nearby lumber shed. The old man soon had a wheelbarrow lined up next to the saw, and was carting the logs away as fast as I could cut them. We carried on in this way for some time, and then he came and shouted in my ear.

'Want a cup of tea?'

'Wouldn't mind!'

'Alright, then. Wait here!'

He disappeared into his house, returning several minutes later with a tray bearing two steaming mugs and some dough-nuts. I switched off the tractor and as the noise faded away the pair of us enjoyed a well-deserved break. It seemed very peaceful in that yard without the din of the engine, and for a while we stood and drank our tea in silence.

'You seem to know quite a lot about this sort of work,' I remarked at length.

'Ought to do,' replied the old man. 'I ran a timber business for forty years.'

'What, here?'

'On this very spot,' he said.

'You've retired now, though, have you?'

'Sent to the knacker's yard, more like.'

'Ah well, you can't work for ever.'

He looked at me. 'Why not?'

'Well . . . er . . . don't know really.'

'I hate not working,' he said, then broke off and glanced towards the lane where a vehicle could be heard approaching. Next moment he was rushing into the lumber shed with the tray and the two empty mugs. I started up the tractor and resumed work just as Mr Pickthall drove into the yard. He pulled up and got out, peering at the much-reduced timber stack, and then at the lumber shed. Eventually, he came over to me.

'Seen my father?' he asked.

'Er . . . who?'

'The old man from the far end of the house.'

'No,' I said. 'I haven't seen anybody.'

'So how did you know the logs had to go in the lumber shed?'

'Just guessed,' I replied. 'All part of the job.'

He looked at me with suspicion for a few moments and then marched into the lumber shed. When he emerged again I was surprised to see he was alone.

'If you do see him,' he said, 'don't let him help you.'

'Righto.'

'I don't want him working any more.'

'OK.'

He glanced at the timber stack. 'You seem to be getting on very quickly.'

'I try my best,' I replied.

After casting me another suspicious look he got into his truck again and drove off. I waited a few more minutes until I was sure he was gone, and then went into the lumber shed to see what had happened to the old man.

'Mr Pickthall?' I called. 'Hello?'

There was no reply apart from a knocking noise beneath my feet. It was quite dark in that shed and I'd assumed I was standing on some sort of wooden floor, but as I stepped back I saw a trapdoor rise up. A moment later the old man climbed out from his hiding place.

'Forty years he's lived here,' he said with triumph. 'And he doesn't know about the hidey-hole.'

'Blimey,' I remarked. 'Quite handy, that.'

'If he'd paid more attention to the business he'd know every nook and cranny by now.'

'Didn't he then?' I asked. 'Pay attention to it?'

'Course not!' said the old man. 'Made me give it up and then ran it into the ground!'

'Why did he make you give it up?'

'For my health.'

'Well,' I said, 'that's a good idea, isn't it?'

'Is it hell!' he snapped. 'All this doing nothing's going to kill me! That's why I have to keep going on long walks, there isn't anything else to do!'

He picked up a stray log and placed it on top of the pile.

'You can carry on helping me if you like,' I said.

'Thank you,' he replied. 'Trouble is, he's likely to come back at any moment.'

'Where does he keep rushing off to then?'

'Oh, don't ask me. He says he's going into buying and selling. You know, auctions and so forth. Damn fool business, that is, if you don't know what you're doing.'

'Well,' I remarked, 'Mr Parker seems to be making a reasonable living from it.'

'Maybe so, but Tommy's got his head screwed on properly. If he puts his money into something, you know it's a safe bet.'

'Suppose so.'

'But that doesn't mean anyone can do it.' The old man looked around the yard and shook his head with disdain. 'Sound business we had here,' he said. 'But now it's all finished.'

Shortly afterwards I went back to the saw and prepared to resume work. The senior Mr Pickthall seemed to have decided he couldn't help me any more, which was a great shame as we made a good team. A few minutes later he gave me a nod and set off walking towards the lake. I looked at the timber stack and realized that in spite of the inroads we'd made during the morning there was still a lot to do. The stack consisted of felled logs, disused beams and broken fence posts, all waiting to be cut up into lengths no shorter than nine inches and no longer than fourteen. I selected an ancient-looking beam and marked it up, then began making the first cut. Suddenly the saw started to produce a strident screeching noise. I pulled the timber away but the noise continued, so I switched off the tractor. Instead of spinning to a halt the blade stopped dead. Then I noticed that there was smoke coming out of the bearings. I placed my hand on them and discovered they were very hot. Cursing slightly, I decided to give the saw time to cool down before trying it again, but I had a sinking feeling that something was seriously amiss. I passed a quarter of an hour carting some more logs into the lumber shed, and then, when there was nothing left to do, I tried starting up once more. Immediately the screeching noise returned and my fears were confirmed: I'd somehow managed to seize the whole thing up. Which was when I remembered the grease gun. Of course! Mr Parker always made a special point of applying grease to all moving parts before and after use, but I'd failed to do it before leaving this morning. Now I had no choice but to pack up and go home. I left the yard as tidy as possible, shovelling the saw-dust into a neat pile at one side, then set off.

Halfway along the lane I met the younger Mr Pickthall returning in his pick-up. I noticed he was carrying four empty oil drums in the back. There was no room to pass so I had to reverse all the way to the yard with him following, and as soon as we arrived he got out and came over to the tractor.

'Where are you going?' he asked.

'Back to Hillhouse.'

'Why?'

'The saw's seized up.'

'But what about my timber?'

'Well,' I said. 'I'll just have to come back another day.'

'I don't want you back another day!' said Mr Pickthall, raising his voice. 'The contract was for immediate completion!'

'Sorry, but I can't see what else I can do.'

'Don't "sorry" me!' he roared. 'I'll be speaking to Mr Parker about this!'

And with that he marched into his house and slammed the door.

Before things went wrong I'd been quite looking forward to the drive back to Hillhouse. Rumbling through hidden country lanes on a tractor would be a pleasant way to end a hard day's work. Instead, all I could think about was Mr Pickthall making an irate phone call to Mr Parker, and then him losing his temper with me. It was one thing being slow on the uptake and clumsy with tins of paint; it was another matter entirely to put a perfectly good piece of machinery out of action. Bryan Webb and the others had warned me countless times about Tommy Parker's temper, and this time I was certain I would be on the receiving end of it. Nonetheless, I had no choice but to go home and face the music.

As if to worsen my plight, the skies darkened and it started raining. There was no cab on the tractor, so by the time I got to Hillhouse I was soaking wet. The painted green square in the gateway looked particularly conspicuous in these conditions, and did nothing to lift the feeling of unease which was descending upon me. I briefly considered the idea of claiming to have been 'rained off' from the timber work, but I soon dismissed this as a feeble excuse. And anyway, the truth would have to come out eventually, so there was no getting away from it.

No one was around when I put the tractor back in the

shed. Mr Parker didn't seem to be back yet and Gail was still at school, so I changed out of my wet clothes, hung them in the boiler room, and continued work on the boats. I tried to remember the last occasion I'd actually been in here doing what I was supposed to be doing. It seemed like ages although it was probably only a few days. With the rain hammering on the shed roof I got quickly back into the swing of things, and soon picked up where I'd left off. This, I decided, was the project I liked best, and in a few days' time I would have the first boat ready for painting. After a bit of hard graft with the electric sander I'd practically forgotten all about the problem with the circular saw. Then the shed door opened and Mr Parker walked in.

8

'Rained off?' he asked.

'Yes . . . Well, no . . . Sort of,' I replied.

He smiled. 'Which?'

'Haven't you spoken to Mr Pickthall then?'

The smile disappeared. 'No, I've only just got back. Why?'

'Well, I seem to have had a bit of trouble with the saw.'

He glanced towards the tractor. 'What sort of trouble?'

'I think it's seized up.'

'But you went round it with the grease gun before you started, didn't you?'

Mr Parker had now begun to examine the saw closely. He placed his hand on the circular blade and tried to give it a spin, but it refused to move.

'No, sorry,' I said. 'I forgot.'

He turned to me sharply. 'Forgot? How could you forget when I've shown you over and over again?'

'Don't know.'

A moment passed, during which I expected Mr Parker to lose his temper. Instead, he simply sighed and shook his head.

'Dear oh dear oh dear,' he said. 'What are we going to do with you?'

I stood in silence as he continued to survey the damage.

The evidence suggested that the bearings had indeed seized up. Vaguely I wondered how much it would cost to replace them, and how long it would take.

'Mr Pickthall's a bit upset 'cos I didn't finish the job,' I ventured at last.

'I'm sure he is,' said Mr Parker. 'And of course I won't be able to send him a full invoice.'

'No, I suppose not.'

He sighed again. 'Bit of a lost day, really, isn't it? Luckily the saw came with a spare set of bearings. You won't go ruining those as well, I hope?'

'No, no. Of course not.'

'Tell you what then, come back after tea and we'll get it fixed.'

'Right. Er . . . what about Mr Pickthall?'

'Don't worry about him.'

'OK . . . thanks.'

I left the shed and headed across the yard feeling quite jaunty. It seemed as if I'd got off fairly lightly. Halfway to the bothy I remembered I had some clothes drying in the boiler room so I cut back to collect them. It was dark now, and as I approached the door I noticed that the light was on inside. Without giving it a second thought I entered and saw Gail standing in her underwear.

'Oops, sorry,' I said, backing out again.

'It's alright,' she said. 'You can come in if you like.'

'Are you sure?'

'Yeah, it's OK.'

I went in and started to collect my clothes from the drying rack, on which now hung most of Gail's school uniform.

'Got caught in the rain,' she said with a smile. 'Just giving it a dry.'

'Oh . . . right. Er . . . haven't you got a dressing gown or anything?'

'Hardly worth it,' she replied. 'Another ten minutes and it'll all be ready.'

'Yes,' I said. 'It does get quite hot in here, doesn't it?'

'Yes.'

In those few moments I couldn't help noticing the whiteness of her brassiere. Also the slight impression it made in the soft flesh of her shoulders. Bundling up my dry clothes I headed for the door. 'Right, bye.'

'Is it alright to bring over some geography homework later?' she asked.

I turned at the door and faced her. 'Well, actually I've been meaning to speak to you about that.'

'Oh yes?'

'Yeah. You see, the thing is, I'm beginning to find it a bit difficult.'

'Why?'

'I just am.'

'But I thought you said it was easy.'

'Well, the homework itself is easy, yeah. But you're growing up very quickly and . . . er . . . I really think you should start trying to do it yourself.'

She shrugged. 'OK then.'

'You don't mind?'

'Course not. I'll be leaving school soon and probably forget it all anyway.'

'Well, I suppose that's one way of looking at it.'

She took her blouse from the rack, slipped it on and began doing up the buttons.

'Tell you what,' she said. 'Why don't you teach me something else instead?'

There were five buttons altogether, not including the one at the top.

'What sort of something?' I asked.

'Give me some darts lessons.'

'Darts?'

'Yeah.'

'What for?'

'So that we can have a game, silly.'

'Oh ... er ... right.'

'We can play up in the hay-loft.'

'I thought that was full of Bryan Webb's hay.'

'It is almost, but he's left a space at one end.'

'What about a dartboard?'

'There's one under your bed in the bothy.'

*   *   *

As soon as I got home I looked under the bed, and sure enough there was a dartboard lying there. It was a red and black model, and I could tell it had been used many times by the number of holes in it. I also noticed a metal tag under the number six, indented with the words: *'Property of Inter-Pub Darts League. Do not remove.'*

I wondered what sort of person would pinch a dartboard from a pub.

By the time I'd had my tea and gone back across to the big shed, Mr Parker had almost finished dismantling the circular saw.

'Need any help?' I asked.

'Bit late for that,' he replied. 'I've practically done it myself.'

His tone wasn't quite as forgiving as it had been earlier, so I took care to make myself as useful as possible. He was about to fit the new bearings, and he got me to hold them in position.

'I suppose you never forget to grease your motorbike,' he remarked, while he tightened up the nuts.

'Try not to,' I replied.

'Well, try not to forget when it's my equipment you're using.'

'No, alright. Sorry about that.'

Half an hour later we had the whole outfit put back together and in full working order.

'Do you want me to go back to Mr Pickthall's tomorrow?' I enquired.

'No,' replied Mr Parker. 'Best let him cool off for a while first.'

'OK, then.'

'By the way, I'm going down to that factory of yours in a day or two.'

'Oh, are you?'

'I bought some more oil drums today, so I've now got enough to make a full load.'

'Oh, well, I hope it works out alright.'

'Yes,' he said. 'It looks like you might have put me onto a good bit of business there.'

This seemed an opportune moment to mention my wages, but then it struck me that Mr Parker had just spent several hours repairing the damage I'd done, so I decided to wait until another time. Instead I went back to the bothy, had a bath and then went out.

I needed to order some more groceries, so before going into the Ring of Bells I stopped at the phone box. As usual there was a long wait before Hodge answered, and then another delay while he went off to find something to write on. This was the fourth or fifth time I'd rung in, and by now I had a more or less fixed list of the items required. The only uncertain element was the biscuits, which I always left until the end. As usual, the selection on offer was very limited.

'Have you got any fig rolls yet?' I asked.

'I'm afraid not,' replied Hodge.

'Custard creams?'

'No.'

'Malted milks?'

'No.'

'Tartan shorties?'

'Wait a minute, I'll go and have a look.'

'OK.'

A minute passed during which the pips went and I had to put another coin in the slot. Then Hodge came back to the phone.

'Did you say Tartan shorties?'

'Yes.'

'Well, we haven't got any.'

'Oh, right,' I said. 'You've got plain digestives, I presume?'

'Yes, we have.'

'Alright then. I'll have those.'

The choice of biscuits generally signified the end of the conversation, but on this occasion Hodge seemed to be waiting expectantly for something else. For my part I said nothing, and meanwhile the moments continued to tick away.

Then at last he spoke. 'You may wish to know we've had a new consignment of beans.'

'Have you?' I said.

'Just come in. Would you like to order some?'

'Baked beans, are they?'

'Yes.'

'Baked beans served with a delicious, rich tomato sauce?'

'Correct.'

'Fresh from the factory, in cans with a handy ring-pull lid?'

'That's the ones,' said Hodge.

'Sorry,' I said. 'I've learnt to do without them.'

At that moment the pips went again and I hung up.

*　　*　　*

I'd been sitting in the Ring of Bells for about ten minutes when Hodge walked in. Giving me barely a nod of recognition he settled down on his usual stool at the counter and ordered a whisky from Cyril.

'Better make it a single,' he remarked. 'Business is a bit slack at the moment.'

It was another quiet night at the Ring of Bells. Outside, the late autumn weather was thickening into a sort of perpetual damp gloom. Inside, the prospect was hardly any brighter. Illumination came from a row of mauve-coloured glass lanterns screwed to the pelmet above the bar. These were supposedly intended to cheer the place up a little, but actually they had the opposite effect. Under their dull glow we sat and stared at our drinks, waiting for the evening to pass.

It seemed unlikely that Hodge would begin one of his stilted conversations with me tonight, given the circumstances, and I expected him just this once to leave me in peace. Consequently I was caught unawares when suddenly he turned in my direction and spoke.

'I gather you didn't get on very well with Mr Pickthall,' he announced.

'Didn't I?' I said.

'Not from what I've been told.'

Hodge had a way of addressing people that meant everyone else in the pub heard it as well, whether they wanted to or not. Apart from him, Cyril and me, there were three or four other drinkers present as well, and as soon as the exchange began I realized that they were all listening with interest. I also saw that I had little choice but to continue.

'Do you mean young Mr Pickthall?' I asked.

'Yes.'

'Well, I wouldn't have said we didn't get on. We just had a minor problem today, that was all.'

'Sounds like more than a minor problem to me,' said Hodge. 'Question of impropriety, I'd have called it.'

'Why?'

'From what I heard you pulled out of a job before it was finished.'

'Yeah,' I said. 'But it couldn't be helped.'

He shook his head. 'I suppose it couldn't be helped when you let down the Packhorse darts team either.'

'Er . . . well, that was a misunderstanding.'

'Oh,' he said. 'A misunderstanding. I see.'

During this conversation Cyril had been busy at work behind the counter, polishing glasses while at the same time attending to what was being said. Now he joined in with a remark of his own. It was directed at me.

'They brought in the Topham's especially for you, you know.'

'Who did?'

'The Packhorse.'

'That wasn't just for me,' I protested.

'Well, no one else drinks it.'

'Oh . . . don't they?'

'Seems a bit ungrateful treating them like that,' he said. 'No wonder they barred you.'

'They didn't bar me.'

'Yes they did. That's why you started coming in here.'

'You can't keep letting people down all the time,' added Hodge. 'Not if you're thinking of starting a milk round.'

'But I haven't said I am.'

'You should be trying to make friends, not going about upsetting people.'

At these words the other customers murmured in agreement.

'Alright,' I said, draining my glass. 'I think I'd better go.'

'But you've only just got here,' said Cyril. 'You can't go yet.'

'Yes I can. Goodnight.'

I headed for the door.

'We're only offering friendly advice,' said Hodge, as I stepped out into the darkness.

'Goodnight,' I repeated.

'Goodnight,' said a chorus of voices from inside. Then the door swung shut behind me.

I stood in the middle of the square recovering from my recent cross-examination, and swore never again to set foot in the Ring of Bells. Which meant, of course, that I was now effectively exiled from both pubs in Millfold.

OK, well, that was no big deal. I would just have to do without drink for the time being, and that didn't bother me in the slightest. After all, there were plenty of other things for me to do. Why should I waste my evenings hanging around in pubs?

I decided to walk back to Hillhouse by way of the lakeside path, and as I passed the Packhorse I glanced over the beer garden wall. From the bottom bar came the sounds of glasses tinkling and raucous laughter, and in the window I thought I saw the silhouette of a man wearing a crown.

Then I turned towards the lake. It was a dark night, but I'd done this walk so many times by now that I could probably have found my way blindfold. The main obstacles were usually provided by the roots of trees straying across the path. However, I'd only had one pint of lager tonight so these didn't present much of a problem. In fact, I hardly took any notice of where I was going at all. Most of the time I found myself thinking about what it would be like if I did indeed start up a milk round, as everyone kept suggesting. For a while it began to seem like an attractive proposition. I quite liked the idea of setting off early in the morning to make my deliveries. There were plenty of potential customers, even though they were spread out a bit, and it would be a good way of getting to know the area properly. Also, if I got the work completed quickly, I'd then have the afternoons free to get on with other things I was interested in, such as looking after Mr Parker's boats.

Something else came to mind as well. I'd almost forgotten about it, but when I was a child I used to help a milkman on his rounds. It was a holiday job, riding around on the back of a milk-float, plonking bottles on doorsteps and bringing back the empties. This milkman had been coming up and down our road for as long as I could remember, and I'd often wondered if he needed a helper. Then one morning he suddenly pulled up while I was riding my bike along the pavement and said, 'Want a job?'

Obviously I'd jumped at the chance, and spent several weeks assisting him until the holidays ended. He always let me do the houses at the end of a row, or at the top of a long flight of steps. Meanwhile he remained with the float and checked off his order book. As far as I knew I was the only kid in the vicinity who was allowed to help him, which gave me a certain amount of local prestige (even though he never actually paid me). If my memory was correct, I had this job the same summer as I'd learnt to row a boat in our local park. All that seemed a long time ago now, but the idea of doing a milk round triggered off some pleasant recollections, so I toyed with it for a while. The reality, of course, was different. How could I set up in business without any capital? For a start I'd need to buy a pick-up (milk-floats were for town suburbs only), and I would have to establish some sort of credit with the dairy which supplied me. Then I'd have to poach all Deakin's customers off him, which as I said before I had no intention of doing. When I thought about it seriously I realized that the whole project was nothing more than a pipe-dream, and as I wandered along in the darkness I decided to forget all about it.

Approaching the water's edge I again heard the cries of seabirds from somewhere out in the middle of the lake. There must have been thousands of them gathered together there, but it struck me at that moment that they all sounded quite lonely. I wondered how far from home they were, and why they'd made this their winter sanctuary. After all, the lake was no calm oasis. The water had grown steadily choppier over the past week, and in daylight hours had a permanent grey look to it. The wind that howled through the trees at night was hardly an inviting prospect either.

Which reminded me: we would have to get the new mooring weight put down soon.

A few days ago Mr Parker had spoken as though this was a matter of the utmost urgency, but since I'd finished building the raft he'd engaged me in a string of other tasks and the job had been put off. When I passed the jetty I stopped to check that the raft was still tethered there safely. It was. I could just about see it in the blackness, gently rocking back and forth.

*   *   *

Next morning Deakin was late with the milk. His usual arrival time came and went but there was no sign of him, and I began to wonder if there was some sort of problem. I didn't bother mentioning the matter to Mr Parker though. He seemed to have something on his mind this morning and wasn't in a very conversational mood. Besides, it was hardly important what time Deakin turned up really, as there was always some spare milk in the fridge. We'd been sitting at the breakfast table for about fifteen minutes when the phone rang. As usual, this caused Gail to rise instantly from her seat.

'I'll get it,' she said, darting into the next room. A moment later she came back.

'Dad, it's for you.'

After Mr Parker had gone to take the call Gail turned to me and said, 'Shall we start practising tonight then?'

'You mean darts?' I asked.

'Yeah.'

'Can if you like.'

'You sure you don't mind?'

'No, course not. Come over about seven.'

She smiled. 'Alright then, thanks.'

Her father came back into the room. 'That was Bryan Webb. He was ringing up to find out if we'd heard from Deakin this morning. He's worried about his Uncle Rupert's homogenized.'

'Blimey,' I said. 'Deakin must be way behind schedule if he hasn't even got to Bryan's yet.'

'That's what I said,' agreed Mr Parker. 'Anyway, I haven't got time to worry about Deakin now. I want to go over to Bryan's and fetch the lorry, so we can load up those oil drums. Then I suppose we'd better get that mooring weight put down before the weather gets any worse.'

'Oh, right,' I said. 'I was going to mention that.'

Instead of acknowledging my remark Mr Parker fell unusually silent, and it again struck me that there must be something on his mind.

It wasn't until well after ten o'clock that Deakin finally arrived, and I saw straight away why he was late: he was

making the deliveries in his ice-cream van. The inside of the
vehicle was laden with milk crates which clinked and rattled
as he came up the hill, heralded by an uncontrolled double
blast of 'Half a pound of treacle'.

Poor Deakin. He had such a harassed look on his face that
I felt quite sorry for him. To get at the milk he had to open
the access door at the back of the van, squeeze inside between
the crates, and then squeeze out again. It looked like a real
struggle, especially since he had so many calls to make.

'Better late than never!' I called by way of encouragement,
as he did a frantic dash across the yard. 'Where's your pick-up
then?'

'Kenneth Turner's giving it a full service,' he replied, dodg-
ing up the steps to the house. 'Otherwise it'll never get
through the winter.'

'Have you spoken to Tommy about the van yet?'

'I haven't had time. Is he here now?'

'No,' I said. 'Should be back later though.'

'Right,' said Deakin. 'As soon as I've got these deliveries
finished I'll come back and see him.'

There seemed to be a certain resolve in the way Deakin
said this, which I thought was a positive sign that he really
did intend to get the matter sorted out at last. Shortly afterwards he was on his way again, charging off down the hill
as the chimes gave yet another rendition of 'Half a pound of
treacle'.

I'd done about an hour's work on the boats when Mr
Parker returned in the lorry and got me to help him load it
up. The top yard was now crowded with oil drums, well over
a hundred, and it took us some time to get them all stacked
and roped. As we worked I noticed that Mr Parker was
becoming increasingly irritable. Loading all those drums was
no easy business, and every time one of them jammed in an
awkward position he would curse under his breath and shove

at it violently until it moved. I couldn't quite understand what was bothering him, so I adopted my usual approach of saying little and making myself as useful as possible. Finally, all the drums were securely tied on the back of the lorry and it was ready to go.

Then, after a brief rest, Mr Parker said, 'Right. We'd better get that mooring weight put down.'

I glanced towards the lake and quickly concluded that this wasn't the best day to do the job. There was a cold wind blowing across the hillside and I could see the tops of the distant trees swaying. Still, I wasn't going to argue with Mr Parker. If he wanted to put the weight down today, then so be it.

The first thing we had to do was transport it to the shore. We couldn't use Mr Parker's pick-up because he'd left it over at Bryan Webb's when he went for the lorry this morning. The tractor still had the saw attached, and the only other vehicle available was the old Morris van parked by the side of the shed. To my surprise it started first time, and he soon had it manoeuvred round to where the weight lay. The van's springs creaked as the two of us struggled to lift the concrete-filled wheel into the back, as well as the accompanying length of chain and mooring buoy. Once again there was a lot of cursing involved as Mr Parker's mood continued to deteriorate, but eventually we got all the gear inside and shut the rear doors. Then we drove slowly towards the lake.

As we approached I saw that the water was still as grey and choppy as it had been yesterday. I looked at the mooring raft as it bobbed up and down beside the jetty, and wondered if it really was as stable as I thought.

Mr Parker seemed to be pondering the same question. He stood on the jetty for a long time looking at the raft, occasionally pressing his foot down on one corner to see how much resistance there was.

'Rocks about a lot, doesn't it?' he said. 'Are you sure you've built it properly?'

'Should be alright,' I replied.

Obviously he needed convincing, so I stepped completely onto the raft to prove I had full confidence in it. To my relief it felt OK, and I was able to move about on the small deck without fear of toppling over.

'We'll need to take one of the oars,' I said. 'So we can guide it.'

Mr Parker unlocked the green hut and tried the door.

'The flaming paint's stuck again,' he said, giving it a pull.

Every time I examined the paintwork on this hut I noticed yet more runs and badly done areas. It certainly was a poor piece of workmanship, and did nothing to improve Mr Parker's humour. Only with a sharp tug did the door come open, after which I went inside and got one of the oars. Then we had the tricky job of transferring the mooring weight (plus the chain) from the van to the raft. It wasn't too bad moving it along the jetty, as we were able to roll it slowly to the end. But getting it from there onto the raft itself was a real battle, accompanied by many more grunts and curses from Mr Parker. We'd just succeeded in getting the weight safely aboard when we heard 'Half a pound of treacle' coming towards us through the trees.

Not now, Deakin, I thought to myself, but there was nothing I could do about it. Next thing the ice-cream van had pulled up by the green hut, where it gave another impromptu blast of its wayward chimes.

'What a flaming racket!' roared Mr Parker, steadying his balance on the mooring raft and keeping well away from the edge. As I looked at his awkward movements it suddenly dawned on me why he was in such an irritable mood. All the signs pointed towards it: for some reason he was afraid of the water. This explained both his distrust of the raft and his lack of interest in the rowing boats. When he was on dry land Tommy Parker bore himself with as much self-assurance as any man I'd ever met. He was strong, independent and successful in business. He could do a thousand and one things that many other people wouldn't even know how to attempt. Yet out here on the water all his confidence just disappeared. Which was obviously why he felt it necessary to shout at Deakin.

'Can't you turn that bloody thing off!' he yelled, as the hapless milkman approached us along the jetty.

'Well, that's what I want to talk to you about,' replied Deakin, with a look of determination on his face.

'We're a bit busy just now,' I said, attempting to defuse the situation. 'Why don't you come back later?'

In order to get away from Deakin I quickly cast off from the jetty, using the oar to propel the raft. Once again the van trumpeted its presence nearby. Suddenly the raft rocked sharply and I realized that Deakin had stepped on board as well.

'What are you doing now?' snapped Mr Parker.

'I'll come with you and give you a hand,' replied Deakin. ''Cos I could do with having a word with you really.'

Mr Parker and Deakin were now holding each other steady. Around their feet lay many yards of mooring chain, and this suddenly caught Deakin's attention.

'Looks like you've got a bit of a tangle there,' he said. 'Let's see if we can get it sorted out.'

He crouched down amongst the chain and began rearranging lengths of it across the raft's deck. I soon realized that there was hardly room for the three of us on board, as well as the mooring weight, the buoy and all that chain. Worse, as we moved away from the shore the lake became noticeably rougher, so that the raft pitched and rolled quite a lot. By the time we'd got far enough out to drop the mooring,

Mr Parker had begun to look very unhappy. He was gripping onto the weight with both hands, and staring down at the black water below. Meanwhile, Deakin continued to fiddle about with the chain, coiling it into loops and so forth, and making some sort of adjustment to the mooring buoy.

'Right,' I said. 'Stand back, Deakin. We're going to let it go now.'

With Mr Parker's help I shoved the mooring weight over the edge. It plummeted into the depths followed by the long, rattling chain, and a moment later it was gone.

So was Deakin.

9

As he shot beneath the surface a surge of water rose up and swirled around our feet. 'No!' cried Mr Parker, arms flailing as he tried to keep his balance. He looked in danger of toppling after Deakin, so I caught him by the hand and the two of us remained swaying there for several seconds, during which time I noticed the mooring buoy floating nearby. There was nothing attached to it.

'He's gone down with the chain!' I said, raising my voice against the breeze. 'Can he swim?'

'Can he hell!' groaned Mr Parker. 'Can you?'

'No, sorry.'

'Well, I bloody can't either!'

A gust of wind battered us and moved away across the lake. The raft was now drifting rapidly, which meant we were already some distance from the spot where Deakin had disappeared. Nevertheless, I kept expecting him to pop up next to us at any moment so we could pull him to safety. It was only after half a minute had gone by that this began to seem increasingly unlikely. Then, on the receding shore, we heard the ice-cream van give a forlorn hoot.

'Do you think there's anything we can do?' asked Mr Parker.

I shook my head. 'No,' I said. 'I think we've lost him.'

'Well, get me off here, could you, please?'

I took the opportunity to let go of his hand, which was

starting to feel rather warm, and retrieved the floating buoy. After that I began paddling back, while Mr Parker strove to maintain his footing. I helped him from the raft onto the jetty, at which point he murmured 'Thank you' and quickly headed for dry land. Then he turned and stood for a long time regarding the lake.

'Dear oh dear oh dear,' he said when I joined him. 'This would have to happen now, wouldn't it? Just when Deakin had found a job he liked.'

I gave no reply but simply shrugged and looked in the same direction, aware that the water now appeared to be much darker than it had before. In the distance a group of seabirds wheeled and turned.

Behind us waited the ice-cream van, with engine running and refrigerator unit whirring loudly. It was a very unnatural noise compared to the wild rushing of the elements, and eventually it succeeded in drawing Mr Parker's attention away from the lake.

I saw him glance round at the vehicle once or twice, then finally he asked, 'Now, what's supposed to be wrong with these chimes?'

'They keep jamming,' I replied. 'That was one of the things Deakin wanted to talk to you about.'

'Well, all he had to do was push the reset button. Let's have a look.'

He climbed into the back of the van, which was now free of milk crates, and reached up to a panel. Then I heard a faint 'click'.

'Try it now, can you?' he said through the serving window.

I leaned into the cab and pressed the control switch. Instantly, the horns on the roof played 'Half a pound of tuppeny rice'. Then there was silence. I pressed it again and got a repeat of the same tune.

'That'll do,' said Mr Parker.

'What about the other bit?' I asked.

'What other bit?'

' "Half a pound of treacle". Shouldn't it play that as well?'

'Oh no,' he said. 'You can only have one or the other. Not both.'

He emerged from the van carrying a bottle of red-topped homogenized milk.

'This was in the fridge,' he announced. 'It must be for Bryan Webb's Uncle Rupert.'

'Oh, right.'

'Could you run it round there quickly?'

'Er . . . if you like, yeah.'

'That's good,' he said. 'It's the least we can do under the circumstances.'

'Yeah, suppose.'

'Ever driven an ice-cream van before?'

'No,' I said. 'Why, are they different from other vehicles?'

'Not too bad, but you've got to watch them on the curves. They can be top-heavy in some conditions.'

'OK, I'll remember that.'

'Maybe you'd like to familiarize yourself with the controls.'

He said this in the form of an order, so obediently I climbed into the cab, from where I watched him wander back towards the water's edge. He went to the end of the jetty and once again stood gazing out over the lake, a motionless figure surrounded by grey, churning waves.

I allowed a suitable length of time to pass, then called through the window, 'Right, I'll get going then!'

Still with his back to me, Mr Parker raised a hand in acknowledgement.

Putting the van into gear I headed off between the trees. The pale afternoon light was beginning to fade already, so when I got to the road I switched on the headlamps. Craning my neck and leaning out of the window I saw that the roof-lights had come on as well. There seemed to be nothing I could do about this, and I had no choice but to drive round to Bryan's place fully illuminated. Despite Mr Parker's warning about top-heaviness the vehicle seemed to handle OK. As a matter of fact it pootled along very nicely, although the steering wheel struck me as being unnecessarily large. On the approach into Millfold it was tempting to set the chimes going, but I had second thoughts when I realized that people might come rushing out to buy ice-creams. Instead I passed through the place in a sedate manner so as not to attract attention.

As I neared Hodge's shop I noticed a large, new sign in the window. I slowed down to have a look.

'SPECIAL OFFER,' the sign said. 'BAKED BEANS REDUCED TO HALF PRICE.'

Continuing on towards Bryan's it occurred to me that I hadn't actually seen or spoken to him since my ban from the Packhorse, and that he might not appreciate me arriving out of the blue like this. After all, he was captain of the darts team I was considered to have let down so badly. What if he'd taken against me like the rest of them, then what would I do? For all I knew he might have been harbouring a serious grudge. Suddenly it didn't seem such a good idea to go turning up on his doorstep, especially as he had all those sheepdogs he could set on me.

Still, I could hardly go back now, so I decided to press on. I pulled into Bryan's yard just as he came out of the house, and was relieved when he gave me a sympathetic smile. As usual he was wearing his cardboard crown.

'Tommy rang up to say you were on your way,' he announced as I got out of the van.

'Oh, right,' I said. 'Did he mention, then . . . about?'

Bryan nodded. 'Yes, he did.'

'Oh . . . right.'

'And you're manning the breach.'

'Yeah, suppose I am. I've brought this.' I handed him the bottle.

'Thanks very much,' he said. 'It's for my Uncle Rupert.'

'Thought so.'

'He likes his homogenized every week.'

'Yes, I remember you saying.'

'In his tea, like.'

'Yes.'

Bryan placed the bottle on a shelf inside his doorway, then turned to me.

'By the way,' he said. 'Tommy asked if you could leave the van here and take his pick-up back.'

'OK then.'

'Save him coming for it.'

'Right.'

This was easier said than done. The Dutch barn which had previously housed Mr Parker's lorry was now home to Bryan's own pick-up and tractor. The other pick-up was parked behind them, and getting it out involved a good deal of manoeuvring. We spent the next five or ten minutes busily forwarding and reversing various vehicles, swapping them all round until the ice-cream van was at the back of the barn and Tommy's pick-up in front. Then the two of us stopped for a bit of a chat.

'Got those boats finished yet?' Bryan asked.

'Well, all the preparations are done,' I replied. 'As soon as I find a spare moment I'll get a start on the actual painting itself.'

'What? You haven't started yet?' He looked quite surprised.

'No, but as I say I'll be getting going very soon.'

'So you'll have them done by Christmas, will you?'

'Oh yes,' I said. 'That should be no problem at all.'

'Be a bit of a push though, won't it? December's almost on us.'

'Well, it hardly matters really. They won't be going back on the water 'til Easter.'

'Maybe not,' he said, giving his crown a significant tap. 'But it's Christmas that counts, isn't it?'

I wasn't sure what he meant by this, so I just nodded and said, 'Yeah, suppose you're right.'

He looked at me for a long moment before a grin slowly appeared on his face. I grinned back and then he laughed and slapped me on the shoulder.

'Good on you!' he said. 'You had me there for a minute!'

I joined in the laughter, and Bryan laughed some more, and then I said I'd better be going.

'Don't be late tomorrow,' he said, as I departed.

'No, alright,' I replied.

Tomorrow being Thursday I assumed he was referring to the next darts fixture in the Packhorse. I took his remark as meaning that my period of exile was over and I could begin drinking there again. This came as quite a relief. My resolution of the previous evening about 'not drinking anywhere for the time being' had seemed very bleak in the cold light of day. After all, what was the point of working if I couldn't go to the pub at night? Now I had confirmation from the darts captain himself: I could go back to the Packhorse tomorrow evening.

In the meantime I had an engagement with Gail to fulfil, so I put my foot down and sped home. When I arrived in the yard at Hillhouse I noticed Deakin's pick-up truck parked in front of the big shed. Standing beside it were Mr Parker and Kenneth Turner, deep in conversation about something or other. When they saw me approach they beckoned me to join them.

'We've had a word with one or two people,' said Mr Parker.

'And we think you might as well take over the milk round straight way.'

'Take it over?'

'Yes, then you'll be all set up to keep it going.'

'Better for everyone in the long run,' added Kenneth. 'People always need milk.'

'Yeah, but . . .' I hesitated. 'Surely I can't just seize control of a going concern?'

'Why not?'

'Well . . . it just doesn't seem right, that's all.'

There was a long silence, then Mr Parker said, 'I thought you liked Deakin.'

'Yes,' I replied. 'I did quite like him.'

'Well, if you took the milk round over you'd be looking after his best interests, wouldn't you?'

'Suppose so, if you put it like that.'

'Nobody would be getting let down.'

'No.'

'So you might as well start straight away, hadn't you?'

I shrugged and nodded towards Deakin's pick-up. 'Is it all fully serviced now?'

'Yep,' said Kenneth. 'OK for another year.'

'And how will I know where to deliver the milk?'

'Deakin's order book is in the cab,' said Mr Parker. 'All the details are there.'

With my head still reeling from the suddenness of this turn of events, I was shown the order book and also a delivery-route map. Kenneth then handed me a wad of requisition dockets for the dairy at Greenbank.

'If you get there early someone'll give you a hand loading the crates,' he said.

'What do you mean by early?' I asked.

'Well, Deakin used to start at five o'clock.'

Five o'clock! This was the part of the equation I hadn't

considered. I always thought I got up early when I worked at the factory, but that was only for an eight o'clock start. Five o'clock was three hours earlier, and I began to wonder what exactly I had let myself in for. To get a full night's sleep of seven hours I would have to go to bed at about half past nine. Which was the time I usually went to the pub. It dawned on me that I was saying goodbye to any social life I had just to keep Deakin's business going. On the other hand, I couldn't help feeling quite elated at the prospect of having my own milk round! I decided to buckle down and get used to the idea of becoming an early riser.

Once everything was settled Mr Parker gave Kenneth a lift home, and I went over to the bothy for some tea. Around seven there came a knock on the door. It was Gail.

'Ready for a lesson then?' she asked.

This made it sound as if she would be teaching me, not the other way round, but I let the remark go and produced the dartboard from under my bed. When Gail saw it she took it from me and seemed to hold it rather fondly in her arms. Then she led the way towards the hay-loft.

'By the way,' I said. 'What are we going to do for darts?'

'There are some up there,' she replied.

Getting into the hay-loft required going up a wooden ladder and through a trapdoor. Gail found the light switch and went up first, and I followed. After clambering over Bryan's hay bales we came to a space about four feet wide and ten long. Just enough room for a darts game. By the time I got there Gail had already hung the board up on a hook at one end. The surrounding area of wall, I noticed, showed signs of having being struck many times by pointed objects. There were also a number of scores chalked up on a nearby plank of wood. Someone had even marked out an oche on the floor.

'Done this before then, have you?' I asked.

'Oh yeah,' she said. 'Loads of times.'

'Who with?'

'Anyone who happened to be here.'

'So I'm not the first one?'

'No, course not.'

She opened a box in the corner and took out some darts. They were a rough-looking bunch with cheap plastic flights, but they would do for practising. She gave me a set of red ones and chose yellow for herself. Then we began.

I suppose we must have played about fifteen games altogether that evening. Gail knew how to stand correctly on the oche, and her aim wasn't too bad. Where she fell down was on tactics. She had no idea about the importance of eights and sixteens for a double finish, nor did she recognize the problem of 'blocking' until it was too late. Time and again she'd be on three darts to win, and then lose the game because she just couldn't see an out-shot. This was were I came in. I was able to give her little hints and tips that I'd picked up over the years, and slowly her play became stronger. At first I won game after game, but after a while Gail began to win a few as well. When she'd had the satisfaction of beating me a few times we gave up for the evening and put the darts away. We both agreed that we might as well leave the board hanging where it was.

'By the way,' I asked. 'Where did it come from?'

'Don't know,' she replied. 'Marco got it from somewhere.'

'Who's Marco?'

'The one who was here before you.'

*   *   *

That night I made the mistake of going to bed early, assuming it was what people did if they had to get up at half past four.

At ten o'clock I was tucked under the sheets with my head on the pillow, but still wide awake. The thought hadn't occurred to me that it would be better to catch up on lost sleep *after* I'd lost it, rather than before. As a result I spent several long hours trying desperately to drift off, while all the time worrying in case I overslept.

Finally, about four o'clock, I got fed up with tossing and turning, so I rose from my bed and put the kettle on. I was bleary-eyed, but began to feel better once I'd worked my way through a whole pot of tea. At twenty to five I went out into the yard, found Deakin's pick-up in the darkness, and set off towards the dairy at Greenbank. I'd never been in that direction before, but it was marked clearly on the map and I was there for five o'clock. As I approached the building a loading bay came into view, where some other vehicles were waiting. There were a few men in overalls standing around, and one of them signalled me to reverse in next to a pile of full crates. By the time I'd got out of the cab he was already swinging them into the back of the pick-up, so I climbed up to lend a hand.

'Morning,' he said, without any introduction. 'Got a docket for me?'

'Oh yes, sorry,' I replied, producing the paperwork from my pocket. 'I'm new to this game.'

'Don't worry,' he grinned. 'You'll soon settle into it.'

I gave him a requisition docket, which he separated in two, giving the bottom half back to me. Then he got me to sign the sheet on his clipboard.

After we'd finished loading he said, 'Right. That's your lot. If you take my advice you'll go down the side of the common first, get rid of your gold-tops, then you'll have an open run for your pasteurized as far as Millfold. After that it should be plain sailing. Oh, don't forget homogenized is on "specials" Wednesdays and Fridays.'

'Thanks,' I said, trying to take it all in.

None of this information meant anything until I got back in the pick-up and studied the order book and route map together. Then I realized that planning a milk round was no less than an applied science. The route included loops, short-cuts and unavoidable dead-ends, but every effort had been made to minimize wasted mileage. As I began making my deliveries I came to understand that the man on the loading bay had spoken with the wise voice of experience. As he'd predicted, the crate of gold-topped (extra cream) milk was empty by the time I'd cleared the common below Greenbank, and I then had an unbroken run of silver-topped pasteurized as far as Millfold.

Nevertheless it was only my first day, and despite the useful advice I soon fell behind schedule. The trouble was that a lot of the delivery points were at the end of remote lanes, and I seemed to waste a lot of time turning round in tiny spaces, and going through endless sets of gates. I quickly came to the conclusion that I would get along much more efficiently if I had an assistant: someone to open gates and plonk bottles on doorsteps while I kept the vehicle moving.

Another problem, of course, was that I frequently got lost. The map was quite detailed but it had obviously been in use for a good while, and as a result some small destinations were lost in the folds. The only way I could complete these deliveries was by guesswork, making random forays up unmarked roads and hoping I'd find the right place eventually. Usually I did, but once or twice I went seriously wrong and had to retrace my journey before trying again.

Less difficult to find was Wainskill, where I had a fair number of drops to do. It was dominated by the ice-cream factory, and quite a few of my customers seemed to live close by. Dawn was breaking as I delivered two pints of milk to the Journeyman, and one each to a small row of dwellings a little further along the road. I wondered in passing if Lesley occupied any of these sleeping households.

By the time I got to the Millfold area I was running very late, but interestingly enough I heard not one word of complaint. Arriving at various farms and business premises I began to recognize familiar faces from the Packhorse (and the Ring of Bells), and in spite of my lateness received nothing but encouragement. In many cases it was obvious that they'd actually been waiting for me to appear with their milk so they could start breakfast. I would have expected this to put them in a bad mood, yet when I finally turned up I was invariably given a cheery wave from the kitchen window. If the door happened to be open I would slip the bottle just inside and say 'Thank you' in a sing-song sort of voice before continuing on my way.

Along the road towards Hillhouse I met the school bus coming in the opposite direction, and as our vehicles passed Maurice sounded his horn in a friendly manner. I thought I saw Gail's face amongst those looking out, but I couldn't be certain.

After making two deliveries at Hillhouse, one to Mr Parker's door and one to my own, the next call was at Stonecroft, which I hadn't visited since the episode with the circular saw. Again there were two drops, one for young Mr Pickthall and a second for his father at the other end of the house. I was hoping to see the old man and maybe have a brief chat, but when I turned round in the yard there was no sign of him. What did catch my eye though, apart from the stack of timber still waiting to be sawn up, was a large collection of oil drums gathered together in one corner. I was just wondering what young Mr Pickthall was planning to do with them all when he emerged from the house, carrying an empty bottle.

'Seen my father on your travels?' he asked in an abrupt tone.

'No, sorry,' I replied, handing him his milk and accepting the empty in return. 'Gone for a walk, has he?'

'Seems like it,' he said, with a grunt of disapproval. 'Half the time I don't know what he's getting up to.'

It struck me that the old man should be free to do as he wished at his age. However, I didn't say anything since it really had nothing to do with me. I wanted to get away quickly before the unfinished timberwork was mentioned, so I nodded politely, and then went off to deliver his father's milk. When I returned to the pick-up I glanced across the yard and saw young Mr Pickthall standing amongst the oil drums, marking each one with a piece of chalk. He looked up as I departed and I gave him a wave, but he failed to acknowledge me.

There were only two or three deliveries left to do after that, yet for some reason I still had a full crate of milk remaining. When I stopped and looked at the order book I realized with a shock that I'd missed out a section of the route! I was supposed to do Bryan Webb's side of the lake first and then come along here afterwards, but for some reason I'd got it the wrong way round. As fast as I could I completed the drops on this side, then tore off towards Bryan's place. He was standing in his yard when I arrived, the cardboard crown upon his head.

'Only an hour and half late,' he said with a grin. 'Not bad for your first day.'

Apparently he'd been watching my progress along the lake from his window, and had already put the kettle on for a pot of tea. This was most welcome as I'd been going continually without a break since before five o'clock.

'Made one or two wrong turns this morning,' I said, as we sat in his kitchen. 'Should be able to speed up though as I get used to it.'

'You could do with an assistant really,' remarked Bryan. 'Deakin's trouble was that he tried to do it all by himself. Want a biscuit?'

'Please.'

He produced a biscuit tin and removed the lid. Inside were fig rolls, malted milks and custard creams. 'Take your pick.'

'Blimey,' I said. 'Where'd you get these from? I can't lay my hands on anything except plain digestives.'

Bryan looked concerned. 'Dealing with Hodgey, are you?' he asked.

'Yeah.'

'And he won't let you have what you want?'

'No.'

'He can be like that with newcomers, can Hodgey. Until he gets to know you a bit better, like.'

'Well, how long does that take?'

'Ooh, it depends,' said Bryan. 'Could be months, could be years.'

'Looks like I'm stuck with digestives then,' I sighed.

'Tell you what,' he said. 'Why don't you let me send in your order? Hodgey won't know the difference and you can collect it from here.'

'Wouldn't you mind?'

'Course not, it's no trouble.'

'What about settling his bill?'

'Oh, don't worry about that. We can sort it out later.'

'OK then,' I said. 'Well, thanks very much. I'll give you my list tomorrow.'

'Alright.'

I stayed at Bryan's another half-hour, sharing tea and biscuits, before I stirred myself. Then I thanked him again and headed home, pleased to have got through the entire circuit without incident. All the milk I'd picked up at five o'clock this morning was now gone. The crates in the rear of the pick-up were full of empty bottles, rinsed and ready for return to the dairy. As I journeyed back I became increasingly aware of the way they rattled and clinked all the time. This was something I'd failed to notice while I was working flat out, but now the sound seemed to follow me incessantly all the way along the lake road and through Millfold. Finally I turned into the gateway at Hillhouse and passed over the painted green square. The rattling ceased as I halted for a few moments, remembering that this was the place I had first met Deakin only a few weeks ago. I got out and looked at the gate I'd been painting that sunny afternoon. How things had changed since then! Now Deakin was gone and I had become the official milkman for Wainskill and Millfold. It occurred to me that it might be a nice idea annually to repaint the square in his memory. He'd been wearing a proper dairyman's overall at the time, and I wondered whether I should think about getting one for myself.

*   *   *

With the rest of the afternoon free I could at last get on with the boats. It seemed like ages since I'd finished preparing them, and now I was quite looking forward to applying some paint. Mr Parker had given me the keys so I let myself into the paint store, selected a couple of brushes, and then went over to the big shed. Inside, the boats were all lined up on their wooden blocks just as I'd left them. I opened a tin of green paint, stirred it, and then began work on the first one.

As I said before, whoever painted these boats originally had done a very thorough job. In all the hours I'd spent with the electric sander, I had only managed to dull down the old paintwork, rather than remove it completely. The first boat's

hull remained a faded but very obvious maroon colour. And
as I began going over it with fresh green paint I began to get
an odd feeling of unease. It was almost as if I was painting
over something irreplaceable. I'd been expecting this part of
the job to be the most satisfying, but I soon found it was
quite the opposite. With every brush stroke the boat looked
less majestic and more mundane. Even worse was when I
had to paint over the gunwales and the curved prow, whose
ancient lines had looked so outstanding in gold. As the old
paintwork disappeared under the new I discovered that I was
rapidly losing interest in the task. After all, my idea had been
to restore these boats to their former glory, not reduce them
to mere tubs. I also realized that I was working at a much
slower rate than I had been at the outset, but put this down
partly to the fact that I was now quite tired, having been up
since the early hours. I was just pondering whether to pack
in for the day when I heard a vehicle arrive outside. Mr
Parker had evidently returned from wherever he'd been, and
a few moments later came into the shed to see how I was
progressing.

'Well,' he said, giving the boat a glance-over. 'The paint
seems to be going on quite nicely, doesn't it?'

'Suppose so,' I replied, without enthusiasm.

'It'll need several coats, won't it?'

'Expect so.'

'Well, don't worry about slapping on as many as it
takes.'

'OK.'

'I've brought back some more chain and a wheel hub,' he
continued. 'So when you've got a moment can you make
up another mooring?'

I wasn't sure when he expected me to 'get a moment'
exactly, but I just said OK again, and watched as he moved
towards the chimney stove in the corner.

'Bit chilly in here,' he remarked. 'I think we'll get this going for you, keep the place nice and warm.'

Next thing we were clearing away the bits and pieces around the stove, and finding suitable pieces of timber to burn. To tell the truth I'd been so preoccupied with the boats that I hadn't noticed how cold the weather had turned. No wonder I felt lethargic and sluggish. In contrast, Tommy Parker seemed to be in a very expansive mood. Soon there were flames darting up from within the stove, and he was making adjustments to the air regulator on the front. As the shed warmed up I began to feel less fed up than I had earlier.

'There you are,' he said, when he'd got the stove going full blast. 'That'll keep it cosy in here.'

'Thanks,' I said.

'I'm off down south with the oil drums tomorrow, so I'll leave you to it.'

'Right.'

Shortly afterwards I had another visitor. Around five o'clock the door opened and Gail came in. I noticed she'd already changed out of her school uniform.

'There's a message for you from Mr Wanless,' she said.

'Who's that then?' I asked.

'You know,' she replied. 'Drives the school bus.'

'You mean Maurice?'

'I've always called him Mr Wanless.'

'Oh . . . right,' I said. 'What's the message?'

'He says it'll be alright to go back to the Packhorse tonight.'

'Ah, that's very good of him. I'll have to buy him a pint.'

Gail looked disappointed. 'Does that mean we won't be able to have any more darts practice?'

'No, no, should be able to squeeze some in, although I'm a bit busy just at the moment.'

'So we will do it again then?'

'Oh yeah,' I said. 'Promise.'

She smiled. 'Thanks.'

I watched her walk to the door and go out, and had to remind myself not for the first time that she was only fifteen. Maybe I should have just said I had no time available to spend with her and left it at that. After all, it would have been practically the truth. Apart from having a milk round to look after and all these boats to paint, there was also a mooring weight to make and put down, as well as a timber contract to complete. On top of all that there was my commitment to the darts team, which seemed rather more important than giving lessons to a teenage girl in a hay-loft. In fact, when I thought about it there was hardly a moment to spare, and now that the shed had warmed up I decided to bash on with the painting for another couple of hours. By seven o'clock I'd got the first coat finished on the boat I was doing and it looked OK, although I remained unhappy about the choice of colour. After that I dashed over to the bothy, had my tea and then went out.

When I arrived at the Packhorse I discovered I'd taken far too much for granted about my status in the darts team. I was made welcome enough, but the demands of the fixture list had obliged them to recruit other players during my absence, and there were no spare places. Bryan Webb bought me a pint and then explained that I would have to play myself back into the side by turning up for future matches on a reserve basis. This sounded fair enough to me, so I sat on a stool in the corner and prepared to watch the action. The visitors tonight were from the Rising Sun, and seemed to be a friendly enough bunch. Unfortunately, they were one of those teams that brought no women with them, so there was nothing much to look at apart from men lobbing darts. The first game was won by the Packhorse, and the second by the Rising Sun. Then suddenly everybody was laughing

about something. I blinked once or twice and saw Bryan and
the rest of them standing in a half-circle, grinning at me and
studying my face.

'Is he or isn't he?' someone said.

'Well, he isn't now, but he definitely was,' said Bryan, and
they all laughed again.

'What's up?' I asked.

'You've just slept through half the match,' he said. 'Watch
out, you're spilling your beer.'

I glanced down. The glass in my hand was lying at a hap-
hazard angle, its contents lapping the rim. Quickly I straight-
ened it, and got up from the stool.

'Blimey,' I said. 'I must be more tired than I thought.'

'Well, you can't burn the candle at both ends,' remarked
Kenneth Turner. 'You'd better go home and get your head
down.'

'Yes, I think I will. Goodnight.'

'Goodnight,' they all chorused as I walked out.

Despite not getting a game of darts, I felt quite good about
my first evening back at the Packhorse. Nobody had said
anything about me 'letting them down' on that previous
occasion, and I assumed from their silence on the subject
that I was forgiven. Now it was just a matter of time before
I was fully accepted as a team member again. The way Bryan
had bought me a pint beforehand suggested that this
wouldn't be too long at all. Feeling fairly contented about
the way things had gone, I wandered back to the bothy and
went straight to bed. I was asleep the moment my head
hit the pillow, waking again at half past four feeling fully
refreshed. After a quick cup of tea I set off in the pick-up,
and realized I was actually looking forward to embarking on
my milk round once more.

As I emerged from the front gate I noticed there was
another early-riser out and about. A figure appeared in the

headlights walking along the road towards Millfold, and I knew instantly that it was old Mr Pickthall.

I pulled up beside him and wound down my window.

'Want a job?' I asked.

10

'Course I want a job,' he said.

'Well, I could do with an assistant.'

'Thought so.'

Without another word he walked round to the passenger's side and got in. I noticed he was carrying a canvas bag from which protruded a Thermos flask.

'You've come prepared then,' I remarked as the journey continued.

'Might as well do it properly if we're going to do it at all.'

'Yeah,' I said. 'Suppose you're right. What about your son though?'

'What about him?'

'Won't he object to you coming with me?'

'None of his business.'

'But what if he finds out?'

'Look,' snapped the old man. 'Do you want my help or not?'

'Of course I do.'

'Well stop going on about him then.'

'Alright,' I said. 'Sorry.'

Having settled the matter we didn't mention it again, but continued driving through the pre-dawn darkness towards Greenbank. We arrived at the dairy bang on five o'clock and I backed straight up to the loading bay, where the men were ready and waiting. It turned out that Mr Pickthall was on nodding terms with a couple of them. They remembered him from the days when he ran his timber yard, and once again I was struck by the way everybody appeared to know everybody else around here. This in its turn helped oil the wheels, and we had the milk crates on board the truck even quicker than the day before. I handed over the requisition docket, signed the sheet, and we were soon on our way again.

What I liked about the old man was that he didn't waste words in pointless conversations. He just rode silently beside me in the passenger seat, peering out through the windscreen at the road ahead and awaiting the opportunity to do some work. Obviously, I didn't ask him to take every bottle of milk to every house we called at: that would have been demanding far too much of him. The gold-tops along the common below Greenbank, for example, I delivered myself, since they were all straightforward drop-offs. It was when we began doing the more remote dwellings that he really came into his own. The first such place had three sets of gates on the entrance drive, all closed, and Mr Pickthall practically leapt out of the pick-up to open them.

'Damn fools,' he said, getting back in after the third gate. 'They don't need them closed at this time of year.'

'Suppose not,' I agreed. I knew nothing about farming, but my assistant seemed to talk with some authority so I took his word for it.

'All the fields are empty,' he added.

Nevertheless, if the customer wanted the gates to be left closed, then we had no choice but to oblige. Mr Pickthall wasn't really bothered either way. He needed something to do, and opening and closing gates was as good a pastime as any. His only complaint was that the people who owned them were 'damn fools'.

Another task cropped up for him when we came to places with awkward-shaped yards. These had been real inconveniences the day before, but with his help they proved to be no problem at all. The procedure was simple. While I did a three-point turn in the truck, he would get out and make the appropriate delivery, returning with the empty bottle just as I completed my manoeuvre. In this efficient way we saved minutes at a time.

It was not yet daylight when we arrived at Wainskill. As we passed the ice-cream factory Mr Pickthall peered through the wrought-iron gates and said, 'So Snaithe finally sold up then.'

'That's what I heard, yes,' I replied.

'Started up from nothing, you know.'

'Really?'

'Same year as I established my sawmill.'

'Oh, right.'

'Good businessman, Snaithe is.'

'Do you know him then?'

'I run into him from time to time, yes,' said Mr Pickthall. 'Last occasion was Whit Monday, 1962, if my memory serves me correctly.'

'Oh . . . er . . . right.'

'Of course, they'd never let him build anything like that these days.'

'Suppose not.'

'Too many planning regulations round here now, you can't build anything.'

'No.'

'Damn fool regulations.'

This long conversation seemed to take its toll of Mr Pickthall and he fell silent for quite some time. Meanwhile, I thought about Mr Parker's big shed and wondered if he'd got planning permission before he built it.

The milk round was going very nicely. We completed the deliveries in Wainskill, and were well on schedule as we approached the Millfold area around a quarter to eight. I'd noticed that the pick-up's fuel gauge was running low. It had a diesel engine, and the only place I knew with a DERV pump was Kenneth Turner's garage, so I pulled in for a refill. Kenneth was already at work underneath a van, which he had jacked up on the service ramp, and he emerged when he heard us arrive. I got out to speak to him, leaving Mr Pickthall in the cab pouring some tea from his Thermos flask. He'd brought two cups along, as well as some jam doughnuts, and had obviously chosen this moment for us to have a tea break. When Kenneth saw him sitting in the passenger seat he gave me a wink and said, 'I see you've got yourself an assistant.'

'Yes,' I said. 'He's been making himself very useful.'

'Well, you can't go far wrong with Mr P. on board.'

'That's the way it seems.'

'Smart boy wanted,' said Kenneth.

After he'd filled the tank I took out some money to pay, but he wouldn't hear of it.

'Might as well put it on account, you'll be needing plenty more after this.'

'Suppose so,' I said. 'Is that alright with you then?'

'Yes, no trouble at all.'

'And I'll settle up in due course.'

'Righto.'

I joined Mr Pickthall in the cab for my tea and doughnuts, and then we pressed on with the deliveries along Bryan Webb's side of the lake. When we arrived in Bryan's yard, he was standing there in his cardboard crown, apparently waiting for us. I took the opportunity to hand over my grocery order, but declined his offer of a cup of tea, explaining that we'd just had one. As we departed again Bryan gave Mr Pickthall a grin and a salute.

'Damn fool,' remarked the old man.

We reached Hillhouse ahead of Deakin's usual time, but I noticed that the lorry-load of oil drums had already gone. Mr Parker did have a very long way to go with them, and he must have decided to make an early start. By now Mr Pickthall appeared to be tiring a little, so it was me who got out and made the delivery. Gail appeared in the doorway just as I came up the steps to the house. She was not yet in her school uniform.

'When are we going up in the hay-loft again?' she asked.

'Pretty soon,' I replied. 'Once I've got used to these hours.'

'Alright then. By the way, my dad's left you some more firewood.' She indicated Mr Parker's pick-up truck, parked next to the big shed. From where we were standing I could just make out some timber piled in the back.

'Oh, right,' I said. 'Thanks.'

She smiled. 'That's OK.'

When I got back in the cab Mr Pickthall was examining the route map.

'Mind if I borrow this?' he said.

'No, of course not,' I replied. 'Any particular reason?'

'I've got a feeling there's a few short-cuts we could make, but I need a bit of time to think them over.'

'Oh, right,' I said. 'You're coming tomorrow then, are you?'

'If you want me to, yes.'

'Well, that'd be fine by me.'

'Right,' he said. 'Then I will.'

We agreed that I would do the last dozen or so deliveries on my own, and I dropped him off just before the entrance to Stonecroft. He cut through a small wicket gate in the hedge, quickly disappearing from view as I continued towards the house. When I got there his son came out to speak to me.

'Seen my father?' he asked.

''Fraid not,' I replied, handing him his milk. 'Maybe he's gone for a walk.'

'Yes, well as long as it is only a walk.' He took the bottle and gave me an empty in return. 'By the way, when are you coming back to finish off that timber contract?'

'Er . . . should be sometime soon,' I said. 'When I get the nod from my boss.'

'Your boss?'

'Yes.'

'I thought you were your own boss now.'

'I am for the milk, yes. But the other things I do for Mr Parker.'

'Sounds like a funny arrangement to me.'

'Does it?'

'Neither one thing nor the other.'

'I'm not that bothered really.'

'No, well, maybe you should be.'

It struck me that this was the type of conversation I usually had with Hodge, a sort of cross-examination with no apparent purpose other than to delve into my personal affairs. I wondered if the two of them ever got together to discuss other people's business. This seemed quite unlikely when I thought about it, as young Mr Pickthall came over as a singularly friendless individual.

It didn't take long to finish the milk round after that, and I was back at Hillhouse by eleven, which I thought was pretty good going. Now I had the rest of the day to get some serious painting done. I took a late breakfast in the bothy, and then went over to the big shed to get the stove lit. Remembering the firewood Gail had mentioned, I stopped by Mr Parker's truck and glanced into the back. To my dismay I saw the abandoned boat from the lower field lying there in pieces. I recognized the broken gunwales, the stern-post and the soft-rotted keel, all piled up ready to burn. With deep misgivings I lifted out two or three fragments, then carried them into the shed.

*   *   *

It took me quite a while to get that stove going. The previous afternoon Mr Parker had managed to kindle a flame in a matter of minutes, after which he'd quickly piled in some additional fuel and closed the lid. Soon it was blazing strongly and required no further attention. By contrast, I had no such instant success. Possibly this was due to my never having lit this kind of stove before, but it seemed more likely to stem from my reluctance to let a once-proud vessel go up in smoke. Time and again I tried, yet failed to get beyond a yellow flicker which would last a few moments before fading away again. None the less, the weather was getting too cold to work without some kind of heating, so I was obliged to persist. Eventually, after several attempts, I tried adjusting the air regulator as Mr Parker had done, and at last the stove roared into life. Then slowly I began feeding the ruined boat into the flames.

*   *   *

Once the shed had started to warm up I chose a brush and prepared to commence work. I'd already got through the first tin of green paint, so I opened another one and stirred the contents. This was a slow task. The cold weather had caused the paint to become very thick and set, and it was going to take a lot of stirring before it could be used. For five minutes I stirred, thinking vaguely of an idea that had evolved during the morning. I stopped and gazed at the green paint, then stirred some more, and the idea came to fruition.

Resolutely, I replaced the lid on the tin and put it back with the others. Next, I went over to the paint store and scanned the shelves. Surely, amongst all these different paints, I would be able to find what I was looking for. After all, only the unlabelled tins were green. One by one I picked up the others and examined them. There were priming paints, zinc paints, emulsions, undercoats and external glosses, in all varieties of colours. I found special yellow paint for use on caterpillar tractors, and red paint for Post Office vans. Some paints had names dreamt up by the manufacturers: Arctic Blue, Eggshell Blue and Deep-sea Blue. Not quite what I was after, but they gave me hope and I continued searching. Somewhere near the back of the store I came across some cardboard boxes, unopened, each containing a dozen tins of paint. I checked the label on the first one. It was Royal Maroon. The second was even better: Burnished Gold. With a feeling of vindication I lifted the boxes down and carried them back to the big shed.

Obviously, Mr Parker couldn't have known he had these paints stashed away in the depths of his store. Otherwise there was no doubt he would have asked me to use them instead of the moribund green. He was probably so busy that he'd lost track of just what he did and didn't have, so by seeking them out I had, in effect, done him a favour. Now the boats could be finished in their proper colours.

I started work straight away, repainting the craft I'd done the day before, then moving on to the next one. The results were so pleasing that I decided to press on into the evening and not bother to go to the pub. This would be the second time in a week that I'd missed going out, but I was sure Bryan and the others would understand. After all, there were no darts fixtures for a day or two, and they were fully aware of the commitments I'd taken on. With these reassuring thoughts in mind I continued applying the maroon paint, and as I did so the boats began gradually to regain their former elegance.

Of course, an alternative way to spend the evening would have been to go up in the hay-loft with Gail. I was half expecting her to appear at any moment and suggest it, but for some reason she didn't, and instead remained alone in the house. Finally, when fatigue caught up with me, I packed my paintbrushes away and went to bed. All in all it had been quite a satisfactory day.

In the dead of night Mr Parker returned. I was woken by an engine and the flash of headlights in the darkness as his lorry pulled into the top yard. I must have drifted straight back to sleep because I heard no other sounds after that.

Next thing I knew, the hour had ticked around to four-thirty and it was time to get up again.

Actually, I was surprised how quickly I'd got used to being an early-riser. Here I was on only my third day as a milkman, making a pot of tea at half past four in the morning as though I'd been doing it for years. I even found myself wondering how people could lie in their beds until six or seven a.m., when instead they could be up and about like me. After all, this was the best part of the day, and nothing could compare with the crunch of cold gravel under my boots as I emerged in the pre-dawn murk.

Someone who was up at the same time, of course, was Mr Pickthall. I found him waiting down on the road, canvas bag in hand.

'Morning,' I said as he slid into the passenger seat.

'You don't have to bother with all that nonsense,' he replied. 'I'm fully aware that it's morning.'

'Oh . . . er . . . yeah, sorry.'

'We've got a job to do and there's no need for idle chit-chat.'

'No, you're right. Sorry.'

'And stop saying sorry!'

'OK.'

'Now then,' he continued. 'I've been having a look at this route map and I've decided that Deakin was taking the wrong road from Wainskill.'

'You know about Deakin then, do you?' I asked.

'Well, of course I know about Deakin!' he snapped. 'Everybody does.'

'Oh . . . do they?'

'Now, do you want to hear my proposal or not?'

'Yes, please.'

'Right.' Mr Pickthall produced the route map and spread it out on his knee. 'I think what we should do is take the upper road out of Wainskill, and then cut through Longridge Scar.'

'I thought that was private property,' I said.

'It is,' he replied 'But it belongs to an old pal of mine and I can square it with him.'

'That's good.'

'Should save us a full six miles by my reckoning.'

'Great.'

'There are a few other minor adjustments as well, but I can show you those as we go.'

'Alright.'

He then lapsed into silence and the journey continued. I was beginning to get used to Mr Pickthall's gruff manner, and had come to the conclusion that it wasn't meant to be personal. On the contrary, it was very kind of him to take such an interest in improving the efficiency of the milk round, and I felt quite grateful. Apart from exchanging the occasional remark about the weather, we travelled on without a further word, arriving at the dairy for five o'clock. The loading-up was soon done and then we were on our way again, working quickly through the gold-top deliveries along the common below Greenbank.

When we got to Wainskill, Mr Pickthall suggested that I did the drop at the Journeyman pub while he dealt with the nearby row of houses.

'Ought to save us a good ten minutes,' he announced, transferring half a dozen bottles into a carrier crate.

'Are you sure you don't mind the extra walk?' I asked.

'I'd say if I did, wouldn't I?' he replied.

'Suppose so.'

'Well, then.'

Next thing he was striding off towards the houses, while I rushed two pints over to the Journeyman. This arrangement certainly helped speed us through Wainskill, and we were soon leaving by way of the so-called 'upper road'. After a mile we came to a turning on the left, with a signpost: 'LONG-RIDGE SCAR'. A second sign said: 'PRIVATE'.

As soon as we'd made the turn I became aware of being surrounded on all sides by something dark and impenetrable. I flicked the headlights onto main beam and saw that we were passing between dense conifer plantations which stood motionless in the gloom.

'Christmas trees,' said Mr Pickthall.

A hundred yards ahead of us a truck was parked beside the road, its reflectors glowing red as we approached. Then I noticed an elderly man working at the edge of the trees. He turned towards us, shielding his eyes from the glare. I dipped the lights while my companion peered out through the windscreen.

'That's a bit of luck,' he said. 'It's the old pal I told you about. Stop here.'

I did as I was ordered and pulled up. Mr Pickthall got out

and slammed the door, addressing a few words to the other man. I was unable to hear what was being said because of the noise of the engine, but next moment the two of them were shaking hands. I could now see that Mr Pickthall's 'old pal' was holding some sort of metal instrument, but I had no idea what it was, nor why he was here in this wilderness at such an hour. Their conversation was brief, and then the two of them glanced towards me. This made me feel as if I was on display in a glass case, but I gave a little wave all the same. In return I received a nod of acknowledgement. Next they wandered over to the trees, examined a few branches between their fingertips, and appeared to concur with each other on some matter. I was just beginning to wonder exactly how long this would go on for when Mr Pickthall returned to the pick-up and got in.

'Alright,' he said. 'That's all settled. We can use this road as often as we like. Drive on.'

There didn't seem to be any question of me meeting our benefactor in person, so after giving him a friendly toot of the horn I set off again.

'By the way,' added Mr Pickthall. 'He says if we're coming through every day we might as well drop him off a pint of milk.'

'Oh, right.'

'Starting tomorrow.'

'OK . . . er . . . What was he doing? I couldn't quite see.'

'He was gauging the trees. Seeing if they're the right size yet.'

'And are they?'

'Not quite. Should be ready in another ten days or so.'

'Just in time for Christmas then?'

Mr Pickthall sighed. 'Well, of course in time for Christmas,' he said. 'No point in growing them otherwise, is there?'

'No,' I replied. 'Suppose not.'

After that I dropped the subject of Christmas trees and

instead concentrated on driving. The short-cut had certainly made a great deal of difference to the journey, and we rejoined the main road almost twenty minutes ahead of schedule.

We were still keeping good time when we arrived at Hillhouse a couple of hours later. To my surprise I saw that the flatbed lorry had already gone from the yard. Presumably this meant that Mr Parker had managed to land some additional business which entailed setting off early, but I had no idea what it might be.

He was still absent when I returned home just before eleven, having dropped Mr Pickthall off at the usual place. It had been another thoroughly agreeable morning, with the old man proving himself more than useful (as well as providing tea and doughnuts).

Now I had the entire afternoon free to do some more painting. In the next few hours I managed to apply second coats to the vessels I'd done the day before, as well as getting started on the next one. The sight of all those Christmas trees waiting to be put on the market had reminded me how quickly time was going by, and spurred me into working at a more productive rate. In fact, I realized that my whole pace of living had gone up a gear, in order to accommodate everything that needed to be done. No sooner had I got back to the bothy that evening than Gail turned up requesting some darts practice. As usual I found it difficult to refuse, and we spent a pleasant hour in the hay-loft making further improvements to her technique. Not until ten o'clock did I finally make it to the Packhorse for a quick pint of Ex before bedtime.

*   *   *

There was no sign of Mr Pickthall's old pal when we cut through Longridge Scar the following morning, and I wasn't sure where to leave his milk.

'Just put it at the side of the road,' suggested Mr Pickthall. 'He'll see it when he turns up.'

'Won't someone take it?' I asked.

'Course not,' he replied. 'No one else comes up here.'

'What about birds pecking the top?'

'There aren't any birds here.'

'Aren't there?'

'None at all.'

'But I thought birds liked trees.'

'Not these trees, they don't. My pal sprays them with every chemical going.'

It occurred to me that this plantation was no less remote than some of the other places we visited each day. The only difference was that there wasn't a doorstep to leave the milk bottle on. So I did as Mr Pickthall suggested and left it at the side of the road.

At least his old pal was an identifiable customer. Most of the early drops we made were to darkened houses containing sleeping strangers. I knew few of the names listed in the order book, and realized that it would take a long time before I became acquainted with them all. Eventually I was going to have to go round collecting the money they owed me, but I decided that this was probably best left until I was fully established.

One client I would always recognize, of course, was Bryan Webb. When we pulled into his yard some two hours later he was wearing his usual cardboard crown. I got out to speak to him, while Mr Pickthall remained in the cab with a look of disapproval on his face.

'I don't think the old lad likes me,' said Bryan.

'It's your crown he doesn't like,' I replied.

'Oh, well, can't be helped. Anyway it's not long now 'til Christmas.'

'No, suppose not.'

'I've got your groceries here.' He stepped into his kitchen and emerged again with a box. 'I took the liberty of ordering you some beans. They weren't on your list but Hodgey's doing them at half price so I thought I'd snap them up.'

'Oh, right, thanks,' I said. 'What biscuits did you get?'

'All of them,' he replied. 'Fig rolls, custard creams, malted milks. That was right, wasn't it?'

'Yeah, that's great. How much do I owe you then?'

'Oh, don't worry about that for the moment. Want a cup of tea?'

'No. Thanks all the same. We'd better keep moving.'

'Righto,' he said. 'By the way, where's Tommy been going off to in his lorry every day?'

'Don't know,' I said. 'Has he gone again this morning then?'

'Yes, I saw him leaving about six o'clock. I could see his headlights.'

'Something to do with oil drums, I think.'

'Oh, well,' said Bryan. 'Tommy always knows a good bit of business when he sees it.'

To tell the truth, I was quite glad that Mr Parker was keeping busy. It meant I could get on with my painting uninterrupted, and with a bit of luck I would have the first boat finished before he saw it. With this in mind I completed the milk round as quickly as possible, said goodbye to Mr Pickthall, and then went home and got the stove going in the big shed. When the place had warmed up a bit I selected a tin of gold paint and started work. I wanted each boat to look perfect, and knew that this part of the job could not be rushed. Therefore, I took great care as I applied my paint-brush to the gunwales, the prow and the stern-post.

It was a process that lasted all afternoon. Outside, the weather had begun to turn very wintry indeed, with flecks of sleet occasionally dashing against the shed's corrugated walls. Inside, however, it was quite cosy and felt like a proper workshop. When I finally stepped back to see the results of my labours, I couldn't have been more pleased. Yes, I thought, a truly professional finish.

I was having my tea in the bothy when I heard Mr Parker return that evening, so I went out into the yard to meet him. On the back of the lorry were about fifty second-hand oil drums.

'It's bloody marvellous what they're doing at that factory,' he said, getting down from the cab. 'Runs like clockwork.'

'Thought you'd be impressed,' I replied.

'They put these old, battered drums in at one end, and when they come out the other end they're fully recon-ditioned. It's like new lamps for old.'

'Yeah, I suppose it is.'

'They've said they'll take as many as I can bring in,' he continued. 'So I've been rushing all over the place chasing them up.'

He seemed to be in an expansive mood, so I said, 'There's a fully reconditioned boat in the shed, awaiting your inspection.'

'That's good,' he replied.

'And the others are in various stages of completion.'

'Well,' he said. 'I haven't really got time to look at them at the moment, if you don't mind. I'm rushed off my feet with all these oil drums.'

'Oh . . . right.'

'So I'll just leave you to it.'

'OK then.'

'As long as the painting's done by Christmas, that's the main thing.'

'Right.'

It was a bit disappointing that Mr Parker didn't want to inspect my handiwork, but I could understand his reasons. A moment passed and then I spoke again.

'Er . . . there was something else I wanted to speak to you about, actually.'

'Oh yes?'

'It's just that I've been putting a lot of hours in on the boats just recently.'

'Suppose you must have been, yes,' he agreed.

'And . . . well, I was wondering if you could let me have some money.'

It was a dark evening, but not dark enough to hide the look of surprise that crossed Mr Parker's face.

'Money?' he asked.

'Yes.'

'What for?'

'So I can pay off my debts.'

'Oh,' he said. 'I see.'

'I wouldn't ask normally,' I explained. 'But the thing is I owe money to Bryan Webb, and I've also got a slate at the Packhorse, an account with Kenneth Turner and another one with Mr Hodge. Oh yes, and one with Deakin.'

'Well, I wouldn't worry too much about that last one,' said Mr Parker.

'No, I suppose not.'

'Plough it back into the business.'

'Alright,' I said. 'But I can't go on much longer like this. I'm used to having a bit of cash on me.'

'You've run out, have you?'

'Practically, yes.'

Mr Parker stood looking at the ground, as if reviewing the conversation we'd just had. Then he looked across at the big shed, up at the sky and down at the ground again. Finally, he spoke.

'Well,' he said. 'I suppose I'd better let you have something to tide you over.'

He reached into his back pocket and produced a wad of twenty-pound notes. Then slowly he peeled one off and handed it to me, placing it in the palm of my hand. A second note followed. Then a third. All this was done in silence, but I could sense that it was causing Mr Parker a certain amount of distress. Nonetheless, I remained holding my hand out, and he continued laying note upon note until I had a hundred pounds.

Then he paused.

'Thanks,' I said.

'Will that settle it?' he asked.

'Yep,' I replied. 'That's fine.'

He counted the rest of his money and returned it to his back pocket before glancing at me again.

'By the way,' he said. 'No one at the factory seems to have heard of you.'

'Don't they?'

'Afraid not. I asked one or two people around the place, but none of them could think who you were.'

'Well, I was only there a few months,' I said. 'Expect they've forgotten me.'

'Yes,' he replied. 'That's what it sounds like.'

11

The Packhorse was through to the second round of the Inter-Pub Darts League. This was the news that greeted me on my next visit, and it seemed to be generally agreed that I'd played a valuable part in the campaign.

'We wouldn't have beaten the Golden Lion without your help,' said Tony as he pulled me a pint of Ex. 'We'll have you back on the team as soon as there's a place.'

'Thanks,' I said.

'Just keep turning up and you're bound to be selected in the end.'

A quick look at the fixture list told me that we were to face the Journeyman again in ten days' time. This was one game I was determined not to miss, so I made a careful note of the date. Then I took my pint and joined the others for darts practice.

In spite of Tony's assurances, I still felt I was a bit of an outsider at the Packhorse, not quite fully accepted. This was in part due to the fact that I always had to leave before closing time, in order to get to bed at a reasonable hour. As a result, I never partook of 'after hours' drinking with Bryan and the rest of them. I was the only one who didn't stay up late, and I couldn't help thinking I was missing out on something. They were all friendly enough, but I remained uncertain about whether they were actually 'friends'.

The same went for old Mr Pickthall, with whom I spent

more time than anyone else. My early-morning companion travelled round with me for hours on end, yet I had no idea if he actually liked my company or not. We made a good team and worked well together, there was no doubt about that, but if I ever made a mistake, for example by taking a wrong turn, he would snap at me and call me a damn fool. Sometimes I wondered if I wasn't a great disappointment to him.

Nonetheless, the milk round was going perfectly. We cut through Longridge Scar daily, picking up an empty milk bottle from the side of the road and replacing it with a full one. Sometimes we caught a glimpse of Mr Pickthall's old pal working amidst the Christmas trees, and he would give us a wave. Then a few more days would pass without a sighting.

Another call we made was to a small detached house in Wainskill. This was a 'special order', Fridays only, for one bottle of homogenized milk. The property lay slightly back from the road, at the end of a cinder path, and I took a liking to it from the very start. Whoever lived there seemed to have found an altogether pleasant spot to call home. A rocking horse carved on the garden gate gave the place a very welcoming look, as did the apple trees and the neat borders. The house itself was in darkness when I made my delivery, but an outside lamp cast a friendly light along the footpath. According to the order book the customer's name was Pemberton, which told me nothing about whether it was a he or a she. A vase of flowers in the window, however, suggested a female presence, and I soon began to get the feeling that this was where Lesley stayed. After all, no one except a young woman living on her own could make a bottle of milk last the whole week. I imagined she led a busy life, and only had time for a quick cup of tea every now and then. The empty bottle on the doorstep, I noticed, was always rinsed to perfection.

Having discovered where Lesley lived, I then realized that the information was of little use since I could hardly go knocking on her door at half past six in the morning. All the same, when I saw her at the forthcoming darts match it would do no harm casually to mention that it was me who delivered her milk.

* * *

We rarely encountered any traffic at this early hour, but one morning on the approach to Millfold a pick-up truck appeared, coming from the opposite direction. As soon as he saw it Mr Pickthall said, 'Watch out, here's John,' and then laid flat across the seat.

Next moment the other vehicle came by and I saw his son sitting behind the wheel. Stacked in the rear were four oil drums. Mr Pickthall the Younger nodded at me briefly, and then he was gone.

My assistant sat up and glanced behind him.

'Is that his name?' I asked. 'John?'

'Yes, we're all Johns in our family,' replied the old man.

'Do you think he was looking for you?'

'I doubt it. He's more interested in some damn-fool scheme with oil drums.'

'Oh,' I said. 'Mr Parker's involved with those as well.'

'I know,' said Mr Pickthall. 'And John's going to run himself into a lot of trouble if he's not careful.'

'Is he?'

'Of course he is. Getting right out of his depth, trying to exploit a market he knows nothing about.'

'Suppose so.'

'Still, perhaps it'll teach him a lesson.'

'Yeah, maybe,' I said. 'Hello, who's this?'

On the road ahead of us was a hitch-hiker, a young bloke about my age, carrying a rucksack. When he saw us coming he stuck out his thumb.

'Don't stop for him,' ordered Mr Pickthall.

'Sorry,' I said, pulling up. 'I always stop for hitch-hikers.'

The young man came to the passenger window, which was a quarter open.

'Going up to Tommy Parker's?' he asked.

'Yeah,' I replied. 'Hop in.'

'There isn't room in here,' said Mr Pickthall, through the opening. 'You'll have to go in the back with the crates.'

This struck me as a bit churlish, but the hitch-hiker didn't seem to mind and had soon clambered aboard. Then we set off again.

'That's the lad I told you about,' muttered the old man. 'We don't want him here, he'll spoil everything.'

'Seems alright to me,' I said. 'Most hitch-hikers are usually OK.'

'Why didn't he walk then? It's only a mile.'

'Don't know.'

'Because he's an idle perisher, that's why.'

Mr Pickthall fell silent and sat glaring through the windscreen, while our passenger rode with us to Hillhouse. I wondered why anyone would choose to turn up here in December. After all, the weather was terrible, and there was nowhere to stay.

'Maybe he's just passing through,' I remarked.

The old man said nothing.

Mr Parker was standing on the back of his lorry coiling ropes when we arrived in the yard. Over the past few days he'd been running all over the place, gathering up more oil drums and taking them down to the factory when he had a full load.

He'd returned from one such trip late the previous evening.

'Now then, Tommy!' called the hitch-hiker from the rear of the pick-up, before leaping down. I noticed he had a rather loud voice.

Mr Parker peered at him for a long moment and then said, 'Oh hello, Mark. You decided to come back then?'

'I said I would, didn't I?'

'Yes, I suppose you did.'

In the meantime I'd got out and delivered the milk. I waited a while to give the newcomer a chance to thank me for the lift. Instead, he ignored me and continued talking to Mr Parker, so I got back into the pick-up.

'Are we going then?' asked Mr Pickthall, with a note of impatience in his voice.

'Er . . . yeah, sure,' I replied, selecting a gear.

As we drove away I saw Gail's face behind the kitchen window, but she wasn't looking at me.

*   *   *

Mr Pickthall said little as we continued the milk round, speaking only when spoken to and giving the bluntest of replies. The arrival of the hitch-hiker had disgruntled him for some reason, and he seemed to be taking it out on me for offering a lift. I couldn't see what difference it made really. After all, as he himself had pointed out, the journey had only been a mile. The guy would have got there anyway, with or without my help. However, the last thing I wanted to do was fall out with Mr Pickthall, so I made no comment on the matter.

Around eleven o'clock I dropped him off at the usual place and said, 'See you tomorrow then.'

He muttered something I couldn't quite hear, and then wandered off towards his home.

When I arrived back at Hillhouse, the kitchen door was wide open. I parked the pick-up and got out just as the hitch-hiker emerged onto the terrace with a coffee cup in his hand. Behind him came Mr Parker.

'Have you got a minute?' he called. 'There's someone I want you to meet.'

I went up the steps and the newcomer was introduced to me as 'Mark'.

'You can call me Marco,' he said.

'Thanks,' I replied. He appeared to have a slightly faded sun tan.

'Mark's going to be staying with you in the bothy,' announced Mr Parker.

'Is he?' I asked, with some surprise.

'Yes. If you don't mind, that is.'

'Well, there's not really enough room.'

'I thought you said there was plenty.'

'When?'

'When you first moved in.'

'Oh,' I said. 'Did I?'

As we talked Marco stood with a sort of sneering grin on his face, looking at me.

'Of course, if it's too much trouble . . .' he said.

'No, it's alright,' I replied. 'I suppose you can have the sofa.'

I expected him to say thanks for this magnanimous gesture, but he merely gazed across at the bothy as if he'd scored some sort of victory.

'That's that settled then,' said Mr Parker. 'Now I must get going. I've some collections to make this afternoon.'

As he walked over towards his lorry, I turned to Marco.

'The door's unlocked, you can let yourself in.'

I was damned if I was going to show him into the place like some kind of estate agent, so instead I went across to the shed and got the stove lit. Then I spent some time giving the boats a look-over. I'd made good progress with the painting during the last week or so, and there was only one boat left to do. All the others were looking pristine in their maroon and gold finish, and I examined them with some pride. Mr Parker still hadn't been in to see them, but I knew he'd be delighted when he finally got round to it.

I needed some breakfast, so I went over to the bothy and found Marco lying sprawled across the sofa. Some of his gear was already spread out on the floor in an untidy manner.

'Been travelling all night?' I asked.

'Yeah,' he said. 'I'm completely fucked.'

'Where've you come from?'

'India.'

'Oh . . . right. Good trip?'

'Yeah, it was cool. But I ran out of money so I had to come back.'

'Did you go overland?'

'No,' he yawned. 'Couldn't be arsed with all that. Flew down.'

'Oh, right.'

He reached into his bag. 'Mind if I smoke?'

'Suppose not.'

Marco lit a cigarette and I opened a window. Then he lapsed into silence, gazing at the opposite wall as he smoked. I got on with making myself some breakfast.

'Have you eaten?' I asked, at length.

'Yeah,' he said. 'Had breakfast with Tommy earlier.'

'So you don't want anything for the time being?'

'No.'

I thought it was a bit cheeky how this Marco kept referring to Mr Parker as 'Tommy', like they were old pals or something. It seemed far too familiar for my liking. After all, he was only some part-timer who happened to have been here before. As far as I knew he'd helped with the rowing boats and done a bit of painting during the summer months, yet the way he went on anyone would have thought he owned the place.

'Incidentally,' I said. 'What are you planning to live on at this time of year?'

'I'll get by,' he replied.

'But I thought you'd run out of money.'

'You don't need money round here.'

'Don't you?'

'Course not. Tommy doesn't charge rent for this place, does he?'

'Er . . . no.'

'Well, then. All you've got to do is run up one or two accounts and you're in clover.'

'You mean with Hodge and people like that?'

'Yeah.'

'But you've got to pay them off eventually, haven't you?'

Marco gave me a long look of disbelief, slowly exhaling as a smirk developed on his face. Then he laughed at me, directly and unashamedly.

'Don't be a cunt all your life,' he said. 'Have a day off.'

*   *   *

There were many signs that Christmas was drawing ever closer. Suddenly all the milk-bottle tops were adorned with tiny sprigs of holly, and advance orders for double cream started to appear on people's doorsteps. It seemed likely that the workload would increase over the coming weeks, so I was glad to have Mr Pickthall's continued assistance. After Marco's arrival I'd half expected the old man to abandon me in disgust, but the following morning he was waiting at the usual place with his canvas bag. I thought it best not to mention the previous day's events at all, and instead pressed on with the milk round as though nothing had happened. This course of action proved successful, and relations quickly returned to normal.

Passing through Longridge Scar it was apparent that at last the Christmas trees had begun to be harvested. Where previously we'd seen only impenetrable darkness, there were now open spaces, lit faintly by scattered brush fires still smouldering at dawn. Not all the trees had gone, however. Whole blocks remained untouched, presumably waiting for the following year, or the year after that. We retrieved an empty milk bottle from the side of the road, left a full one in its place, and continued our journey.

When I next delivered to the house with the rocking horse on the garden gate, I thought there might be a note asking for extras during the festive season. There wasn't, but nonetheless I decided to leave a complimentary tub of cream as a goodwill gesture. This caused Mr Pickthall to murmur that 'One customer was no better than the next', and that any tradesman who gave produce away free of charge needed his head examining.

Each afternoon went by in the comparative sanctuary of the big shed. With the stove lit and the door closed, I continued work on the final boat uninterrupted. I'd really enjoyed doing this project over the past few weeks, and speculated about what Mr Parker had lined up for me next. Something interesting, no doubt, but I rarely got a chance to speak to him as he was always so busy with the oil drums.

One evening, however, I met him coming across the yard just after he'd returned from a short trip in his lorry.

'You won't forget there's still that mooring to make, will you?' he said.

'No, OK,' I replied. 'The lake seems a bit rough for putting it down though.'

'You could maybe have a go at doing it next week,' he suggested. 'The weatherman says we're in for a calm spell.'

'Oh, right.'

'Get Mark to lend you a hand.'

'OK.'

The idea of Mark (or 'Marco' as he preferred to call himself) lending anyone a hand seemed most unlikely. He was quite easily the laziest person I had ever met. Not only did he sleep half the day, getting up ages after I'd finished the milk round, but then he just lounged around in the bothy for hours on end, smoking with the window closed and helping himself to my biscuits. Never did he offer to make a pot of tea or anything like that, even though he knew I was busy. His excuse was that he 'couldn't be arsed', although I noticed he always managed to pour himself a cup if I went to the trouble of making some.

Despite all this, Gail seemed to think he was highly fascinating. She was forever turning up at the bothy on pretexts, such as looking at Marco's photographs from India. These were interesting enough in themselves, I suppose, but they only needed to be seen once. Not three times.

At one point I asked him what he thought of the place and he said, 'Brilliant, but you probably wouldn't like it.'

'Why not?' I asked.

'You just wouldn't,' he replied. 'You're the wrong type of person.'

Marco had a very unfortunate way of putting things, but all the same I realized that if we were going to have to share then I might as well try and be friendly. For this reason I asked him if he fancied coming with me to the Packhorse.

'What, and spend the evening with "ye yokels"?' he said. 'No thanks.'

'Actually, they're a good crowd,' I remarked. 'They're going to put me on the darts team.'

'Lucky you.'

'We're playing the Journeyman tonight.'

Marco leaned back and looked at the ceiling. 'Oh the excitement!' he said. 'I can hardly bear it!'

'So you don't want to come then?' I asked.

'No,' he replied. 'I think I might go and see if young Gail wants to come out to play.'

I didn't like the sound of this, but I was hardly in a position to do anything about it. Instead, I had a bath and got ready to go out. As I did so I thought about Bryan, Kenneth, Maurice, Tony and the rest of them, and wondered if they'd appreciate being referred to as 'yokels'.

When I got to the Packhorse I saw that someone had been busy getting ready for Christmas. In a half-barrel outside the door stood a tree decorated with tinsel, while bright fairy lights shone at all the windows. Down in the bottom bar the mood was similarly jolly. The home team practised with their darts, drank beer and waited for the visitors to arrive. I ordered a pint from Tony and then went and spoke to Bryan, who was giving the scoreboard a wipe with a damp cloth. His crown was on his head as usual, but in the festive surroundings it no longer looked out of place.

'Evening, Bryan,' I said. 'You're looking very seasonal all of a sudden.'

'Yes, I suppose I am,' he replied. 'Tell you what, though, it's been a hell of a year in between.'

A few moments passed as the meaning of his words sunk in.

'Have you been wearing it for a whole year then?' I asked.

'Course I have,' he said. 'That's the bet.'

'What bet?'

'The one I've got with Tommy.'

'Sorry,' I said. 'I don't know anything about a bet.'

Bryan gave me a surprised look.

'But you must have heard,' he said. 'It's public knowledge round here. Tommy bet me I wouldn't wear my crown from one Christmas to the next.'

'Oh,' I said, smiling. 'I see.'

'And I bet him he'd never find a use for all that green paint he bought.'

'Well, there was rather a lot of it,' I remarked.

'Yes,' said Bryan. 'I thought I was on to a winner until you turned up.'

'Me?'

'Yes.'

'What difference did I make?'

'You saved Tommy's bacon, didn't you?' he said. 'Once you got going on those boats I didn't stand a chance.'

There was a flurry of movement around the door, and a new group joined the throng. It was the team from the Journeyman, and as they bustled in Bryan went over to greet them. Trying not to think about what he'd just said, I got some darts and took a few practice shots at the board. As I did so I realized that there was no sign of Lesley. For some reason she was late, and I assumed she would be arriving shortly. In the meantime, the two sides were drawn up, and preparations made for the first game. Only then did I discover that I hadn't been selected.

'We've decided you're not quite ready yet,' explained Tony. 'But don't worry, it's only a matter of time.'

'So I'll get on the team eventually, will I?' I asked.

'Of course,' he said. 'Eventually.'

From beneath the counter he then produced a number of

cardboard crowns, all folded flat. 'Do me a favour and hand these round, will you?'

The crowns were made to the same pattern as Bryan's. I passed amongst the players giving them out, and kept one for myself. It was gold, with three prongs. Bryan chose a new silver one to replace the old one on his head.

'Might as well be comfortable,' he remarked with a grin.

I didn't enjoy the evening very much, despite having being given a yuletide crown to wear. I watched the darts without any sense of involvement, and as one game followed another it gradually dawned on me that Lesley wasn't going to turn up. When I went for another beer I asked Tony if he knew where she was.

'Oh, we won't be seeing her for a good while,' he replied. 'She's gone off on her travels.'

'Has she?'

'Yes' he said. 'Decided there was more to life than playing darts every night. She's gone overseas, I think.' He handed me my pint. 'By the way, this one's paid for, courtesy of your boss.'

For the first time I realized that Tommy Parker was present in the Packhorse. Glancing through to the top bar I saw him standing with the landlord and his cronies. He gave me a nod and I raised my glass in thanks. It felt like a consolation prize.

*   *   *

Sometime later a cheer went up, signalling that the home side had won the match. As hands were shaken and darts put away, I spoke to Tony about paying off my slate. He took a notebook from beside the till and studied it for a few moments.

'Right,' he said. 'Forty-one pounds and ninepence I make it. Call it forty for luck.'

'Oh . . . OK,' I said. 'Thanks.'

'Do you want to pay your darts subs while we're at it?'

This turned out to be another tenner, and apparently covered the cost of the sandwiches which I'd always assumed were free. By the time I'd sought out Kenneth and Bryan, and paid what I owed them, I had less than ten quid left. I thought about my outstanding debt with Hodge and realized that, despite all my hard work, I was more or less skint. Not until I went round collecting the milk money would I have any cash again, and that'd have to wait until after Christmas.

'Oh, I meant to tell you,' said Bryan. 'My Uncle Rupert sends his regards.'

'Does he?' I replied. 'Er, right . . . thanks.'

'Very impressed with how early you're delivering his milk.'

'Is he one of my customers then?'

'Of course he is,' Bryan grinned. 'You know his place. Out at Wainskill. Got a rocking horse on the garden gate.'

A bell rang.

It was last orders at the Packhorse, but as usual no one took the slightest bit of notice. The darts team had won yet another victory, and they were now in celebratory mood. As a result, I was the only person actually to leave at closing time. I slipped out of the door and walked across the square past the Ring of Bells. Through the window I could see the gloomy minority seated round the bar. Everything seemed to be the same as it always had been. Then I headed home in the darkness, still wearing my pretend crown.

When I arrived back at Hillhouse I noticed that the light was on in the hay-loft. It was well past Gail's bedtime, but I guessed she must have been up there with Marco all evening.

Entering the bothy I contemplated the untidiness he'd created. His clothes and bedding were lying all over the place, and on the table were unwashed cups and plates. I looked in my biscuit tin and found that it was completely empty. Even the plain digestives had gone. I was too tired to clear up now, so I went straight to bed and fell asleep immediately.

Some time later Marco came back, making no attempt to be quiet. He fiddled about for ages with his bag, taking stuff out and putting it back in again, until he heard me stir.

'Oh, you're awake are you?' he said.

'No,' I replied.

'Enjoy the match?'

'It was alright.'

I heard him light a cigarette, and then he said, 'I've been getting a bit of practice in myself.'

'Have you?' I asked.

'Yeah.' There seemed to be a sneer in his voice again. 'From what I've heard you spend all your time playing round the outside.'

'Well, yes,' I said. 'That's the best way to start, isn't it?'

Now he was smirking audibly. 'No, my son, you've got it all wrong. You should have gone straight for the bull's-eye.'

*   *   *

When I got back from the milk round next morning I saw Deakin's ice-cream van parked in the yard. Beside it stood Bryan Webb. It was usually a pleasure to see Bryan, but on this occasion the sight of him made me very uneasy, especially as he was wearing his silver crown.

'Morning,' I said, attempting to sound cheerful. 'Tommy not around?'

'He's inside making a phone call,' replied Bryan.

'Oh, right. What brings you here then?'

'I've come to have a look at these boats,' he said. 'It's only a formality, of course. I know I've lost the bet.'

'What was the stake?' I asked. 'Just out of interest.'

'If I won I could choose anything out of the big shed. If I lost I had to wear my crown for another year. As a sort of penance.'

'Is that why you picked a new one?'

'Yes,' he sighed. 'Come on then, let's get it over with.'

We walked over to the shed and I slid open the door, revealing the line of newly painted boats.

When he saw them Bryan turned pale.

'Oh dear,' he said. 'Oh dear oh dear oh dear.'

'They were supposed to be green, were they?' I asked in a resigned way.

He nodded. 'Tommy'll blow his top.'

While Bryan stood gazing at the boats in stunned silence, I gave the paintwork an inspection. Running my hands along the gunwales and over the prows, I concluded that the job I'd done was perfect. Unfortunately, I'd used the wrong paint.

Next moment I heard Mr Parker's boots scuffing the gravel as he approached from across the yard. I braced myself when he entered the shed, knowing that this time he really would lose his temper.

And lose his temper he did. The displays I'd seen on previous occasions were nothing compared to this. He took one look at the boats, and then his face turned from pink to purple.

'Flaming hell!' he roared. 'Now what have you done?'

'Well . . .' I tried, but it was no good, he wasn't listening.

'Are you trying to ruin me or something? Ever since you came here it's been one thing after another! Paint spilt all over the place! Machinery wrecked! You cost me a contract up the road, and then go and charge me a hundred pounds

... a hundred pounds! ... to tart up these bloody old tubs! What the hell do you think this is, a flaming bottomless pit?'

He turned towards Bryan, who was still muttering 'Dear oh dear' to himself.

'Alright, Bryan! You've beaten me fair and square! So what are you going to take? Eh? How about my tractor? Or my welding gear? Come on, take your pick! There's lots to choose from!'

'It's alright, Tommy,' Bryan managed to say.

'No, it's not alright!' cried Mr Parker. 'You've got to have something! Tell you what, you can take one of these bloody boats off my hands! Here!'

He seized hold of the nearest boat and started hauling it towards the door single-handedly. The sudden exertion made the veins stand out in his neck, so that it looked as if he would do himself an injury. For this reason I grabbed the other side to lend a hand. I winced as the boat came off its wooden blocks, and scraped across the concrete.

'Tommy,' pleaded Bryan.

Mr Parker ignored him and kept heaving with all his might.

'Tommy!'

We drew nearer to the door. Beyond it lay the loading ramp and the gravel yard.

'Tommy!' Bryan tried again. 'Tommy ... please, listen ... I don't want a boat ... really, I don't ... look, there's something else I can take.'

*   *   *

Ten minutes later, Bryan rode away on my motorbike. We watched as he crossed the yard and descended towards the front gate, still wearing his cardboard crown.

Then Mr Parker turned to me.

'Well now,' he said. 'That's that settled nicely, isn't it?'

'Suppose so,' I replied.

'You hardly ever used it anyway.'

'No.'

'So it might as well go to a new home.'

'Yeah.'

By this time his mood had returned to normal, and he seemed content to give the boats their long-awaited examination.

'You've done a good job there,' he conceded. 'But I think we'll have them painted green all the same, if you don't mind.'

'Oh . . . OK then.'

'It'll give you something to do for the rest of the winter.'

'Right.'

'And after that Mark can take over.'

'Mark?'

'Yes.'

'What's he going to do with them?'

'Mark always looks after the boats in the summer. He's just the right type of person for the job.'

'But what about me?'

'Well,' said Mr Parker. 'To tell the truth I had you in mind for selling a few ice-creams.'

I stayed in the shed until about half past two, but did nothing more than open a tin of paint, stir the contents and replace the lid again. The rest of the time I spent gazing at the boats, while I considered my options.

Finally, I emerged into the pale afternoon light and stood looking across the yard. The lorry-load of oil drums had gone, which meant that I had the whole place to myself.

Almost.

I glanced towards the bothy, where Marco lay sleeping behind drawn curtains. Then I started the concrete mixer, and prepared a length of galvanized chain.